Blueberry Muffins Are Up A Buck A Pair

By
Starmel Spring & Leroy Henry

www.blueberrymuffins.org

Blueberry Muffins Are Up A Buck A Pair
www.blueberrymuffins.org
© Copyright 2015 by Leroy Skeers & Richard Hodgert

ISBN: 978-1-62967-052-2
Library of Congress Control Number: 2015950103

Cover design by Tatiana Villa
Cover art illustrated by Starmel Spring & Leroy Henry
Interior design by Veronica Yager

Published by Wise Media Group, Morro Bay, California
www.wisemediagroup.com

NOTE TO READER ON OPTIONAL SOUNDTRACK

Dear Reader,

Music was a huge part of our inspiration during the writing of this book and created such a wonderful atmosphere. Thanks to Spotify, that same music is available so you can enjoy a great soundtrack to read by with playlists curated for each chapter. Sometimes you'll find that the music ties in directly to the theme while at other times it simply sets the right mood.

Each chapter contains a QR code. If you have a camera and QR application on your smart device (tablet, smart phone, etc.), you can load the playlist by simply taking a snapshot of the QR code at the start of each chapter and you will be redirected to the playlist on Spotify.

If you don't have a device capable of reading QR codes, you can still access the playlists for each chapter by visiting:

http://www.blueberrymuffins.org/soundtrack.html

Try it now:

 *Spotify is free to listen to, but does require registration. If you want to listen without advertisements, they also offer a premium ad-free option.

We hope you enjoy!

DEDICATION

"Blueberry Muffins Are Up A Buck A Pair" is dedicated to my best friend and co-author, Richard Hodgert (Starmel Spring) who passed Feb 26, 2013. It all started on Halloween night in 1973 at my record shop in the University District in Seattle from this humorous quip of Richard's. We were so inspired and galvanized by his remark that we started the book that very night and spent many long evenings into the wee hours over the next three years completing it. We were only 20 years old when we began. The original manuscript sat in storage for decades until Richard's passing.

With the new e-book technology available in 2014, I decided to finish editing the manuscript and publish the book in his honor. Richard was like a brother to me and we shared so many great experiences over our forty plus years of close friendship. Writing in close quarters in our early twenties was very special and I'll always be grateful for our creative partnership. We had already spent the previous five years, since we were fifteen, writing songs together, so this was not a big stretch for us.

I would like to thank Richard's wife Amy, my wife Bonnie, our daughter Kelsey plus all our friends and family who have shown love and support for this project. And last but not least, Mrs. McKillop who dutifully typed up the original manuscript.

Thank you to Brian Schwartz of Wise Media Group for his wonderful guidance as well as Veronica Yager and Tatiana Villa. You have all helped turn this lifelong project into a reality.

Richard, here's to you. Writing this book has really been a blast and now we can finally share it with the public - as you first envisioned. And I agree with you - that Blueberry Muffins would make one heck of a movie.

—Leroy Henry

CONTENTS

CHAPTER ONE

BLUEBERRY MUFFINS

It seems like 1959
Yet somehow amongst us
So far into the future
It's come back behind

"Time to get up, Albert!" ignited Martha the maid as she flung some good ol' Dr. Corncob's Grits into the skillet. She didn't realize how strange she appeared this morning with her steaming red face and those curlers popping out the side of her head.

Upstairs, Albert was already up. In fact, he was always awake and hadn't been to sleep since he was seven. That's what he credited to his seventy-seven years of seemingly infinite youthfulness and vitality. Everyone admired the old boy but nobody believed or understood his behavior, so he simply avoided explanations.

Albert twisted up the radio volume to the chorus of Blueberry Muffins, a song that had been one of his favorites through a lifetime, an oldie but goodie...

> *Blueberry muffins are up a buck a pair*
> *Newspapers bloom in time square*
> *Time, time, time*
> *That's a laugh and a half*
> *Time is a common point of view*
> *So here's looking at you*

Flipping the radio switch at the song's conclusion, Albert rocked back and forth to the beat of his heart while fully absorbing the sunrise.

Albert, you see, was a janitor (a custodial engineer he jokingly preferred to be labeled) at the neighborhood elementary school where he could most easily communicate and relate with pleasurable abundance. Looking forward to seeing all his young friends was sure nice but the work had become such a tedious routine.

Totally engrossed in hoping that today would somehow be different, Albert tightened up his suspenders and slipped on his wingtips. Locking the bedroom door behind him, he slid down the bannister and lunged into the kitchen.

"Time and time again, I've pleaded with you, Martha. No more grits!" Albert emphasized tensely, peering gravely into the frying pan. Martha sunk into the corner, laughing at the wall while listening to Albert's foot-stomps fading down the hall.

Quickly returning with his soiled maintenance cap and Space Scouts lunchpail, Albert planted a sloppy kiss on Martha's receding forehead and hastily slammed the back door behind him.

He was met with the usual sound of loudmouthed over-actives exchanging important, detailed nothings at the bus stop across the street. Albert sure got a kick out of the youngsters. While crossing behind a passing bakery truck on its morning rounds, he scanned the mob of kids, failing to locate Wilber, his seven-year old associate and number one best friend.

"Hey Albert," Porker called out, mischievously removing something from his lunch pail. "Want my muffin?" Albert was somewhat hesitant. Porker was usually alright but you could never tell, especially in front of the others, showing off and all.

"Ah, Albert where you been? These are blueberry muffins!" Porker exclaimed as he extended the muffin out to Albert.

Albert's eyes gleamed as he happily caved in. "Ok, ok, I guess," he offered as he took a huge bite and winked facetiously, rubbing his belly around and around. "Hey thanks a lot, Porker," Albert sputtered with his cheeks full and bits of muffin spraying out. He laughed in pure delight with his mouth twisted wide open, goofing around. Taking another healthy chomp, Albert noticed this one to be a lot more crunchy and couldn't quite manage to keep it all in his mouth. Part of it was dangling out and all the kids were pointing at him and jumping up and down in hysterics.

Albert croaked, "A worm, a worm!" and ran off, stumbling up the driveway, past Martha's vintage Packard, toward the house. He landed hard on the back porch and sat there brewing for awhile with strange ideas shooting through his mind until he suddenly thrust backwards in an explosion of laughter. "Just wait, Porker, just wait!"

Martha squeezed her head out the kitchen window with her eyebrows on the upswing. "What's all the commotion about, Albert? Hurry up now before you miss the school bus!"

"Don't worry, Martha. I haven't forgotten," Albert said in exasperation. He picked himself up, burying his hands deeply into his pockets and crisply returned to the bus stop. But nobody was around! No one. "Great, the janitor shows up late for school again," Albert chuckled to himself and began the long and lonely trek to school. However, he had only gone a couple blocks when he heard the familiar sound of a bus roaring up behind him.

Trotting back, he waited as the bus rolled up with the brakes squeaking and the kids' faces smashed up against the steamy windows. It was most certainly a different substitute driver this morning who swung the doors open as Albert hopped up the steps and quickly sat down in the first seat behind the driver, too embarrassed to even look back. He didn't feel like talking to anybody anyhow. His mind just kept revolving past how many times that Porker had been involved in tricking him.

An unusual quietness was holding tightly this morning. But every few minutes, a faint and strange mumbling could be heard. Albert didn't really comprehend what he was hearing or seeing though and gently closed his eyes, transfixed by the constant rumble and whirl of the bus wheels.

Suddenly, the bus driver laid on the horn, snapping Albert out of his daze. The dog-eared driver veered the bus erratically, over-steering the entrance to the school, propelling past the school grounds and zipping around the bend! With his best smirk, Albert jerked around approvingly only to discover that all those school kids... were actually senior citizens along for a picnic outing!! They waved at him in unison while the conductor in the back of the bus, dressed in a pristine, white baker's uniform and chef hat, wound his pocket watch. "Nice day, huh Albert?"

Mystified, Albert unsurely examined the driver who guffawed wildly, mastering the controls. In the rear view mirror, Albert caught a glimpse of the conductor repositioning his mask. "Just relax and have a good time, Albert."

Albert elected to let it all go and apply a cool composure. Contently settled back in his seat with his arms folded, he watched the countryside miles flash by as he whistled assuringly to the tune of Blueberry Muffins, dreamily closing his eyes and beginning to drift away...

CHAPTER TWO

PEOPLE FLOATING IN THE PARK

The bus abruptly jerked to a halt, ricocheting Albert out into the aisle. A distinguished looking English gentleman, twirling his umbrella, waited to board as Albert skipped hurriedly down the bus steps.

"Jolly good morning, wouldn't you say?" claimed the gent as he tipped his derby hat. The door sealed shut and the bus rolled away, leaving Albert in amazement of the most astounding park he had ever witnessed.

Albert worked his way through rows and rows of animal shaped topiary, winding deeper and deeper into the inner workings of the park, feeling totally enthused and content. He was especially glad that he hadn't made it to school after all. Settling himself into the shade of a grandfather birch tree, Albert fixed his

eyes down the rolling hillside. The whole park seemed
to be a parade of paradise.

The queen was fishing for monkeys
Smoking flowers and smiling at the sky
A midget dwarf claps frenziedly
Dancing in the trees and peeping for a hide

Smiling flowers and laughing birches
Chuckling squirrels make crazy lurches
All is fun under the hysterical sun
As people drift to the sky, one by one

A hot rain showers
Rainbows fall from the wind
Time to laugh proclaim the flowers
Pulling in their petals and releasing a grin

Underneath a flowing fountain
An old dalmatian sits in a pool
Playing his white grand piano
Keeping his charm and cool

The grandmaster sits and plays
An old favorite tune
For a friend on his birthday
That is coming up soon

A parade of penguins
Parachute out of the sky
To watch Monopoly's performance
As Albert skips on by

See the petrified horses
Sliding around again
Wall to wall smiles
On all of them

Hopping leap-froggers nudge away
Stemming recognition of the hour
Eyeing the chiming clock
Atop the brick tower

Everyone rolling like candy wrappers
Down whatever comes their way
Avoiding penny pinching leap-froggers
Begging to get through the day

See the old woman sitting still
Peering from the thickest shade
Watching the little girls run
Oh, the way they jumped and played

See the pies on the tablecloth
Spread open on the grass
Today is the town gathering
For the children of the past

See the rabbit-faced patrolman
Shaking shaky hands
Lecturing the early showing
On their youthful demands

"Don't go chasing rainbows after dreams of distant gold"
The young oldsters were told
Still being chased all over the place
By the patrolman with the rabbit face

Albert broke himself away from the crowds, wandering down a sidewalk that wound deeply into the park. The wind was whistling through the orchard where peacocks spread calmly on the lawn. A few people were seen chatting lightly and investigating mossy statues just ahead, in a very peaceful and enchanting aura.

Drifting off the sidewalk onto a path over several small, rolling hills, the grass was much higher here, swaying waist high. Music from the park could still be heard off in the exterior and sweet streams of fragrance blew in with the breeze. Albert scissored his way through the wild grass that now towered over his head and forged on, mumbling to himself and turning over the change in his pockets. He soon came upon an opening in the grass and stood before a plank door at the foot of a small mountain.

Becoming very curious, Albert pinched an eye through a keyhole, straining harder to see what lay beyond. He raised his fist and tapped gently on the door. A geezer answered in a very startled fashion. Covering his mouth, the geezer gasped, "We're not open," and quickly closed the door.

He then reopened the door just a hair after a few seconds and pondered, "But we're not exactly closed either." The geezer scratched his little head in bewilderment as he motioned Albert to come in. "Shhhh," the geezer hushed, as a faceless face swept by, leaving only a trailing voice behind. "Welcome to the Lavender Lava Mountain Room."

Orange, puffy clouds floated by ever so slowly and Albert could still very faintly hear the echoes of sound from the park. Yellow and maroon vapors appeared from the geezer's breath when he exhaled. Off in the distance, Albert could see some very odd kind of mechanical people with green and blue heads, laughing and walking slowly and crooked. They seemed to be headed toward a village in the center of the hollow mountain at the end of hundreds of steps leading down to it that appeared to be made of black and white ivory, like that of an enormous grand piano keyboard.

Albert navigated through his hazy thoughts and cautiously trailed well behind the blue dwarves who wandered off into the distance beyond the eastern shadows of the mountain walls and down the ivory staircase. The wanderers had grown quite thin as Albert finally approached the head of this musical staircase and hesitated. "Come on, old timer," a group of villagers from below encouraged, their voices reflecting rather mushily off the lavender mountain walls. "Come along and follow us."

And so, Albert began his distant descent, sinking into the first ivory step, sending walls of music pumping out with majestic sensations. As he negotiated each step downward, the cathedral air became more and more absorbing. A crescendo built as the steps fell anxiously behind him in awkward momentum. Hobbling down the scale in rhythm, Albert noted the hurried pace of the others several motions into the distance.

Movements upon movements unveiled quite quickly, dismissing any possibilities of resting any time soon. As Albert scurried down and neared the bottom of this grand staircase, the air became oddly very thick with thoughts upon thoughts clustering in his head. Huge overtones continued to resonate and roar from the piano staircase, echoing off into the valley.

Albert was motioned into the down-sloping mouth of the heart shaped valley to where long rows of picnic tables centered in the middle of a glen. All the villagers stood gazing into the pink skyline as a flurry of kaleidoscope skyballs hailed down from above, casting music to play an Anthem For A New Day, as was their daily morning ritual.

These villagers were known as the Euphorians and before their morning meal, they faithfully harmonized as one to the heartbeat of the sun. As Albert marched down the steep incline closer to the glen, he observed the Euphorians toasting in unison to this new day. They held their crystal refreshments of sunflower juice high in glory. Albert could definitely feel their warmth, health and splendor start to overwhelm him as he moved in even closer.

Suspended in the dawning skyline, the kaleidoscope skyballs concluded the anthem in an ultra round of acceptance from the Euphorians as they cheered and clapped, beginning to find their way to be properly seated at the tables. Rolling over carpeted aisles between rows of picnic tables, the kitchen maids pushed their table carts full of nourishing breakfast. They wore yellow sunbonnets and aprons and seemed to shine with a sweet, churchly radiance as they blessed the young ones who yawned.

One of the kitchen maids broke away from the others and sauntered very gracefully over to Albert. She curtsied in the soft-coated wind and gently grabbed him by the hand, leading him to one of the long breakfast tables to be seated for this morning's meal.

Suddenly there was a commotion and all the kids sprung to life as Mr. Pepclapper, the local rep from the Sticky Candy Company, worked his way through the crowd. He tossed handfuls of bars out to the kids from his long, out of shape arms, hiding them in small hands. Mr. Pepclapper merrily skipped his way throughout the breakfast tables, encouraging the excited little ones to eat and letting them touch his enormous hands.

Albert's eyes were magnetically sealed to the breakfast glassware as he listened to all the off the wall philosophies and babbling in this strange Euphorian language. As he gazed further into the distortions of the glassware, the conversations whistled across the grass and into the Zoological Gardens nearby where odd sorts of speckled and tinted species grazed under a grove of Jade trees.

The Zoological Gardens portrayed a true sense of peace where fluorescent feathered birds spread their wings wide, opening wonders of design. Two-headed zebras pranced near a stream of morning sunlight while a few Euphorian children played croquet off in the distance.

Albert excused himself from the table and nudged his way through the congregation and out into the open sunlight, finding his way down toward the village entrance. He slowly edged along the cobblestone block where lonely dogs barked and the bells of the village steeple chimed. Glancing back, Albert sighted several villagers picking themselves up from the breakfast tables and drifting away.

Continuing onward, Albert spied a parked taxi with its engine idling and the driver aimlessly snoozing away. A Cadillac was parked in front of the cab. A gum-chewing lady uncorked her head out the car window with her horn-rimmed sunglasses reflecting Albert's face. She said, "Waiting has never bothered me before but could you please spare a minute? I'm looking for a small boy heading home from the park on his bicycle. Have you by chance seen him? Have you seen my little Herman?"

The woman continued staring insanely at Albert who sharply rotated his head back forth in negatory fashion. "No ma'am, I have not seen your Herman," he responded.

"Well anyway," the lady quibbled, "I want to take my son to visit the barber. His hair has been dying steadily since his last science music experiment failed. If you see him, please tell him to go visit the barber, ok?"

"Will do," Albert reassured her and gestured politely by tipping his cap.

Suddenly the lady turned blue with fright, locking the car doors and rolling up the windows hurriedly. She pointed frantically down the block to warn Albert and sped off.

> They came rolling from down the street
> Huge rubber heads and tiny little feet
> They laughed and smiled
> As in they filed
> Hundreds and millions
> Thousands and billions
> They all looked the same to me
> As I entered the town

They all wore a frown
Turning and crying
All seemingly dying
For they were afraid to meet
An out of town man
So they turned around
And rolled away or ran

Albert whipped around and bounced up some steps to the porch of Uncle Zach's General Store and burst in, slamming the door behind him. 'Heads of rolling rubber!" Albert blurted out.

Uncle Zach looked back over his shoulder, all stooped over. He stroked his day-old beard, chewing on a good wad of gum and without even losing a beat he professed, "They come from hidden caves in the shadows of the Lavender Lava Mountain walls. Curious, that's all, curiosity."

Albert stood wobbling his head back and forth in disbelief, staring out the window as the storekeeper returned back to tend to his dusting. "So, where ya been and where ya from?" he asked Albert while lightly wiggling his ears.

"Centrifugal Drive," Albert declared. "The name's Albert."

"Nice of you to visit us here, Albert," replied Zach.

Albert turned around just in time to catch the storekeeper heading downstairs. "I must go down to the cellar now to feed the rats," Zach chuckled. "Best way to keep them out of the store is by feeding them down there." The storekeeper quickly yo-yoed his eyebrows, "Now if you'll please excuse me."

"Well, good luck," Albert hollered back as he opened the door and backed his way down the porch steps to the sidewalk. He was immediately blindsided. In obscure collision, a bicycle and its former occupant toppled to the sidewalk. Reaching down, Albert pulled the bicycle off the youngster. "I hope the three of us are ok," Albert joked to the boy.

Checking out the apparatus, Albert swung his leg over the seat. "Mind if I test her out and see if she's ok?" he asked.

"Why not? You earned it," quipped the boy, rubbing his knees and elbows.

Albert pushed off and wheeled away with the youngster trotting along the back side. "Nice piece of machinery you have here," remarked Albert as he pedaled harder, trying to increase his speed to keep the bike from wobbling.

"Yeah, designed it and built it all by myself," the boy bragged.

"Where did you get all the money to do this?" quizzed Albert.

"I work for myself as an inventor in the sciences of transportation," the boy proudly administered.

"You don't say," pondered Albert. "How much do you want for it?"

"Ah, I guess you can just have it, sir," offered the precocious boy. "It's just a matter of science. Please take it. And besides, I need to go visit the barber."

Albert skidded the bicycle to a stop. "Well then, you must be Herman, I presume? Your mother is worried about you and wants to make sure you get your hair cut, ok?" Albert extended his hand, "I'm Albert, and you, my friend, are a very fine scientist. Thank you, Herman."

Albert pushed away and coasted down the hillside, away from the village and toward the far mountain caves at the beginning of the horizon. As Albert made his way from the village, the Euphorians lent tender hands in friendship, waving goodbye as Albert disappeared into the shadows.

Prismatic roads lengthened outward beyond the reaching of the beating colors of the sun spectrum. On both sides, large overhanging cliffs dared to swallow Albert as he coasted through dim caves, leaving cells of inner space lurking in the chillness. Purple tints of hot steam rose steadily from large crevices upon the many peaceful faces of an oncoming parade of travelers. The last of whom played a long, ivory flute to the varieties of their marching.

As the bicycle bounced over this rough terrain, Albert clutched tightly onto the handlebar grips. He rolled on with a soft breeze that began to rustle through his long, white hair, signifying an opening not far into the bleakness. He turned over the pedals quickly and rhythmically, guiding his new bicycle toward the daylight.

Soon coming to the mouth of the mountain, Albert exited and found himself in the emptiness of a broken country road. He became momentarily confused as to which direction to go before reasoning that downhill would be much, much closer and clearly the best direction. Over his shoulder, Albert captured all his great memories of the day so far as he faced the onrushing atmosphere.

Albert rode easily in a wide-eyed, half unconscious state, listening to the sunbirds fluttering above his head, stimulating a series of daydreams that made time glide by effortlessly. Casually riding handless, he deeply gazed at the pale blue sky and the way the figurine clouds floated in and out of imaginative designs as he worked into the transition of the mid afternoon. The autumn weather had come around slowly this year and the early October sun was still readily available and very welcomed.

Just then, an oncoming tractor sent Albert sprawling off the road and into a cornfield. Filling the air with his now ever present bombardment of laughter, he gathered himself up from beneath the bicycle. Slowly getting up, Albert dusted off his trousers and began to walk down the tall aisles of corn. Steeply on his tiptoes, he strained to reach a huge husk of corn at the top before coming to a sudden freeze. Peeking between two stalks of corn,

Albert noticed a man in a fancy fedora hat and a woman wearing a long dress of soft crimson sipping tea under an umbrella table.

Albert decided it would be a good idea to let the couple have their privacy and quietly sneaked his bicycle down the aisle of corn to the end. Gazing outward, he took in a breathtaking meadow surrounded by a forest of balloon trees, many spotted in shades of marmalade sunset.

Albert eyeballed a quaint little country lane that cut between the cornfield and balloon plantation and again pushed off, continuing the most amazing adventure of the day. Many farmhouses were spotted on the horizon as he swiftly emerged into the entrance of the plantation. Popping noises were heard all over yonder as several small characters came into view.

The plantation kids were picking balloons for the circus that was coming soon. In the atmosphere that crackled and popped, the faster pickers raved and cackled in helium voices as they carefully tiptoed through the patch, selecting just the right balloons. Masses of wisecracks were floating through the plantation air as the kids prepared their harvest for the Traveling Circus From Outer Space that was landing in town for the weekend.

As Albert guided his bicycle down the lane between rows of balloon trees, the flat-faced children stood on the fence waving grateful hellos and goodbyes. "See you at the circus, mister," they giggled as Albert waved his final farewells and focused on the upcoming bend. He wasn't too sure how to get out of this place but trusted his instincts enough to go along with the flow so he kept pedaling through the grove of balloons. Just around the bend, a plantation foreman came out of nowhere in a truck full of freshly harvested balloons tied down and quickly applied the brakes.

Albert asked for directions and the foreman pointed him off in the right direction down a bike path heading west, straight into the afternoon sun between more and more endless rows of balloon trees. The roundabout table of time was revolving ever so slowly and through the mechanics of trial and error, over the past ten minutes or so, Albert had now mastered the pathway. It was becoming more narrow now as the trees thickened and Albert could sense he was nearing the end of the grove as he tunneled his way underneath the colorful, arching branches overhead.

As he rounded the final bend and emerged from a thicket, Albert came upon an intersection of pathways. He could go left. He could consider heading right. Or he could chance going straight ahead through a small, somewhat inviting but mysterious tunnel. It was calling out to his better intuition. Albert sensed he should continue his pursuit of going west toward the sun and forged ahead through what appeared to be a very, very long tunnel.

It seemed like the right decision and so off Albert went. He pedaled through the darkened tunnel for what must have been a good quarter mile when he noticed a door coming up on his left side. Albert stopped and pondered the possibilities. A yellow sign hung over the door that cautioned, "Emergency Exit Only."

Albert took a deep breath, contemplating the risk factors. He'd always seen these mysterious doors in tunnels all his life but was always in a car or bus going way too fast or else he was just simply too occupied to notice or care much. He could not recall anyone ever caring or mentioning anything about doors in tunnels. It was just an accepted fact. Giving it further thought, he'd actually never seen anyone use these doors either. It did catch his attention once when he drove by a door and noticed it cracked wide open. What the heck were these doors for anyway? And what was behind them? After all, it's only a tunnel and all people want to do in a tunnel is get to the end as soon as possible, right?

Dismounting from the bicycle, Albert decided to take a peek and put an end to this lifelong mystery. Clutching at the heavy door, he pulled hard to budge it open and slowly cracked it open a little more, just enough to poke his head through and take a gander. A truck barreled by, startling Albert out of his peaceful mindset he had been locked into for most of the day. Then, oddly enough, a school bus lumbered by with the kids' faces smashed up against the windows. This was the tunnel to Centrifugal Drive! Albert knew this bus! As it made its way through the tunnel, he could faintly make out a figure in the shadows at the rear of the bus. It distinctly looked like that of the Conductor waving goodbye. The kids were coming home from school and Albert knew exactly where he was.

"So, this is where that door goes!" Albert proclaimed to himself. "I had no idea. Wait until I get home and tell Wilber."

Albert negotiated his new fangled bicycle through the tunnel door and onto the sidewalk and turned for the ride homeward. He leaned back in his seat, now feeling very ingenious and very enriched for the day he had experienced. Barreling through the tunnel, everything went black for just a moment and then Albert shot through a blanket of light at the end. Alas, ahead was a glorious sight to behold - a sign for Centrifugal Drive. Man, what a welcome sign it was.

He hung a right on Centrifugal Drive and picked up more and more speed as the anticipation of going home mounted. Just up ahead was the old school and as Albert had suspected, it was long deserted. Everyone had gone home except the librarian, Miss Rosegarden, whose car was still there all alone in the parking lot.

Albert could see her bobbing head in the window, planting books on the shelves. She was wearing her old-fashioned green, ankle length dress, as was always her custom on this day of the week. She was quite a pleasant person, like most librarians but sort of mysterious and most definitely resembled a certain character in a novel she had recently authored.

Albert tightened the brakes and slowed considerably as he continued down Centrifugal Drive. It was time to wind her down now and put an end to this very long and memorable day as he rolled by all the familiar houses he had known all his life. On this autumn day, the evening was starting to settle in and it seemed as though almost all the neighbors had moved. The old neighborhood was indeed very lifeless and uncomfortably still.

Before he knew it, Albert was home, turning down his driveway and being met by his beloved mongrel dog, Columbus who raced out to greet him, jumping up and down, soaking Albert's face and getting in some extra licks. "Now get down, boy," Albert instructed Columbus as though he were talking to a little human. "I've had a rather wild day. Let's go inside and I'll tell you all about it."

Dinner was steaming off the table as Albert slipped nonchalantly into the house as if it was just another day. Maid Martha was sitting alone in her favorite seat at the table, her reflection beating off her empty plate in loud silence. Without so much as moving a fraction, she piped, "Albert, you're seven minutes late for supper. I thought something had happened to you!"

"Sorry Martha," shrugged Albert, only half listening as he took his place across the table from Martha, quickly reeling in the mashed potatoes.

The truth to the matter being, Albert was late in coming home at least once a week and his excuses always seemed to be a little peculiar and offbeat. Sometimes as Albert tried to explain things to Martha, she would just shake her head, withholding a tempting smile and walk away to do the dishes or something.

But tonight, Albert ate away without explaining much at all, a somewhat preoccupied stare in his eyes. Martha, upon observing this, helped him to seconds and watched him promptly gorge that down too.

Gradually, Albert got up from the table, "A very good meal to you, Martha," he offered before bounding up the stairs three steps at a time to his bedroom. Closing the door behind him, Albert snapped around as he heard a sudden tapping at his bedroom window.

"Wilber! How the heck are you?" asked Albert as he raced over to help his young associate in. Wilber very often came to see Albert by climbing up to the garage roof and in through the window.

"How's it going?" grunted Wilber, squeezing through the window opening. "Didn't see you at school today. What gives?"

"Missed the bus," began Albert slowly. "It's a very long, short story," chuckled Albert. "Hey, did you remember? The Traveling Circus From Outer Space is expected in tomorrow morning!"

"Unreal!" croaked Wilber, scratching his head in disbelief. "Maybe I can snag a job dealing popcorn and get in free."

"You know, it looks like the elves will be out tonight at Mr. Silverton's," Albert estimated as he glared up at the moon. "Maybe we can make a little circus money!" (He and Wilber were paid handsomely to keep the colony of Nerschvinkle Wenchneck elves off Mr. Silverton's next door estate because they had been frequently devouring the zillionaire's prize roses)

"The Nerschvinkle Wenchnecks will be out tonight, for sure" Wilber proclaimed. I'll meet you at Old Man Mulberry's Maltshop at midnight, sharp, ok?"

"Solid," echoed Albert. "And do remember to bring the things on the list," Albert reminded Wilber.

"Over and out," Wilber deliberated, disappearing out the window and down the drainpipe. Albert proudly watched the highly intelligent seven year old slip into the darkness.

CHAPTER THREE

THE NERSCHVINKLE WENCHNECKS

Albert figured he might as well go down to the malt shop a little early and write a bit until Wilber showed up. So, he sharpened up a few pencils and fetched his notebook out of his closet. A note caught the corner of his eye. It was from Newton N. Newton, the third, another one of the intellectual seven year olds that Albert hung out with.

> *Albert, try these on for size! My latest*
> *invention = platform roller skate shoes.*
> *Just flick the easy switch and the rubber*
> *wheels will freeze and become the*
> *soles of your shoes.*
> *— Newton*

Albert removed his wingtips and then slipped his feet into his new platform roller skates. He tested them out, pacing around the bedroom, trying to get used to their extreme elevation. They were actually pretty comfortable as shoes too. He grabbed his notebook, crawled out his bedroom window onto the garage roof and slid down the drain pipe.

He knelt down, unlatching the freeze lever on the roller skates and started off easily down the sidewalk toward Old Man Mulberry's Malt Shop. This was one of the mutual hangouts for many of the neighborhood kids from the school. Being the janitor, he was quite popular with most of them. But tonight he hoped that Porker Clark would not be among them.

Gliding rhythmically now, under the pale amber streetlights, Albert could hear the Nerschvinkle Wenchnecks chattering about. Every so often, one of the elves would even dash past him unexpectedly and then disappear into the bushes.

With his former style of skating finally coming back to him from his youth, Albert managed to pick up speed and ease his way the three blocks to the maltshop almost effortlessly. Albert rounded the corner beautifully just like an old pro and sighted Mulberry's just down the street a bit with the neon signs blinking on and off in florescent, hypnotic pinks and greens.

Closer by the stride, Albert recognized some of the schoolboys involved in a comic book trading session.

It appeared to be another indication that the Traveling Circus From Outer Space would indeed be landing tomorrow morning on Saturday. Hoping to keep the new roller skate shoes a secret, Albert locked down the wheels and flung open the door. The scene inside was only too typical. A lot of Wilber's classmates were buzzing around and chatting over Mulberry's malts in all of those delicious flavors and colors.

There was Old Man Mulberry back in the corner, standing unsteadily on a bar stool changing a lightbulb - eyeglasses sliding down his nose. Albert headed to the back towards his favorite booth where he liked to write so much.

"Hey Mull, what's the scoop tonight?" Albert joked with Old Man Mulberry.

"Circus Kaleidoscope, as a matter of fact, and word has it, they'll be arriving in town tomorrow morning! Want to try some?" asked Mull, peering over his loose wire rim glasses.

"Try what?!" Albert inquired.

"Doctor Corncob's Circus Kaleidoscope Ice Cream! Just got it in a few minutes ago, special delivery, you might say," winked Mull.

"For sure!" Albert blurted. "How often does this happen?" he reasoned.

"Alright, Albert, I'll get you some. Coming right up," Mull gestured. Albert plopped himself up against the back of his favorite booth and pulled his notebook and favorite pencil out of his backpack. A lot of folks were pretty curious about what he was up to, always carrying around that old backpack and notebook. Albert had been writing more and more recently, reflecting back on his seventy-seven years. Poems always had been a great form of relaxation for him and besides, it would be nice picking up a few bucks by submitting his writings to Mr. Silverton's prestigious magazine, "Planetary Digest."

Veronica, the tight-eyed waitress with the most dazzling, twinkling eyes, approached, "Good evening, Albert. Coffee?"

"Sure thing, thanks. And lots of it, Veronica, please."

Veronica giggled, "And I'll have some of our fresh, Doctor Corncob's Circus Kaleidoscope coming right up! It's got everyone really super revved up for the circus tomorrow. Bye-bye, I'll be back in a flash," she winked.

Albert heard an excited voice coming up the sidewalk and sure enough, it was Wilber spurting through the door with a brand spanking new copy of Doctor Corncob's Fantasy Magazine for Schoolboys. A look of true inspiration centered in Wilber's eyes. "Albert, I just caught a glimpse of the latest edition and it's for certain now, The Traveling Circus From Outer Space opens at 10 in the morning!"

"Oh, and check this out," Wilber added, "See inside for entry blanks for the Star Zip Trip. I'll read the instructions."

STAR ZIP TRIP

*In so many words or less, write why
you'd like to tour the galaxies
with The Traveling Circus From Outer Space
and then come back the day before you left.
Deposit the box top entry inside a
self-addressed stamped envelope
with your picture on the back and drop it off
at your favorite neighborhood post office.
(Offer valid in participating galaxies only)*

Albert opened his notebook to the answer he had been working on for a few weeks now. He and Wilber had studied secretly and independently on crafting their answers.

Albert's answer for the contest was shaping up like this. "I would like to tour with The Traveling Circus From Outer Space because once when I was a child, I thought the stars were reachable and touchable. I never once lost hope that the future would ever find us. Once when I was lost, I looked beyond the other side of the sky until I heard the circus calling me back from deep inside."

Albert looked across the table to Wilber, "You got your answer yet?"

"Finished!" bragged Wilber as both planted their answers into the secret envelopes. "Come on, Albert. Let's drop these off at the post office on the way back to Mr. Silverton's. The Nerschvinkle Wenchneck elves are really chattering tonight. I could hear them all the way from my house."

Albert slapped down some change on the counter by the cash register and led the way back outside, being met by a stiff breeze. It was now drizzling slightly and turning into a misty night as some splotchy clouds crept in and out of the moonlight. The sky was of intense interest tonight as both Albert and Wilber dawdled down the sidewalk, looking up anxiously, hoping to catch sight of The Traveling Circus From Outer Space.

Albert and Wilber soon made it the few blocks back to Mr. Silverton's, walking through the iron gates of the huge estate and up the long driveway. Mr. Silverton, sure enough, was standing visibly from the third story terrace of his monstrous white mansion. It looked as though he were singing as he bobbed around, moving his hands in expression. It wasn't until the boys were below him did the zillionaire notice them and promptly toss down a couple of Energized Chocolate Bars from his velvet smoking jacket.

Wilber instantly ripped off the wrapper and took a crunch. "Sounds like the elves are very plentiful tonight," Mr. Silverton.

"Correct, Wilber," informed Milton, smiling underneath his snow white mustache. "They are out there, very much out there, and plucking my prize roses, I might add."

"Come on out here, Milty," Albert suggested.

"No, no I can't possibly," puffed Milton. "Tonight is the night of the Zillionaire's Midnight Ball and I am being honored." He stopped and quickly caught his breath. "So, you see fellows, I couldn't possibly join you. Now remember, get to work and you'll get ten cents a minute plus a reward if you happen to catch me one. Good luck and go get 'em, men!" Milton chuckled as he waved his college pennant and retreated gallantly into his study.

The boys disappeared around the back side of the mansion. Reaching the other side, they stood surveying the entirety. They could see mostly everything but only within a limited distance as the drizzle mounted. The two quietly sneaked towards the grove of trees, hoping to startle an elf and catch one off-guard. Down a long embankment, weaving in and out of the tree trunks, Wilber suddenly spotted an elf, a Nerschvinkle Wenchneck!

Wilber motioned to Albert and whispered, "You take the right diametric angle and the cutback, surround approach. I'll head the other way."

Over rolling mounds of lawn, ducking in and out behind majestic rose bushes, Albert carefully crept closer to the elf, quietly signaling Wilber by flashing his arms as they closed in from opposite sides. The dimness was now changing as the moon started to peek around the fragmented clouds. Albert and Wilber crept by way of a thin slice of moonlight, drawing closer now to the small object, now seeing that it was in fact a Nerschvinkle Wenchneck napping carelessly beneath a birdbath.

Wilber caught Albert's attention in the pale moonlight and finger-mapped a course of strategy. Wilber instantly split right as Albert doubled around, sneaking to the left. Waiting until the moment was just right, Albert charged and jumped onto the elf. It somehow wriggled away, only to run squarely into Wilber coming full force from the other side. Wilber held the elf cautiously by a pointed, blue ear. "Thought you'd get away, did you?"

Albert unfolded off the ground. "Nice maneuvering, Wilber. And as for you, Mr. Nerschvinkle Wenchneck, nice try. We're going to tie you up and present you to Mr. Silverton He'll teach you a little lesson on trespassing and eating his prize roses!"

Albert and Wilber had never actually caught an elf before and so they of course, were very thrilled and pleasantly surprised to be in this situation.

"Well, you've certainly taught me a valuable lesson and have given me an ear full!" exclaimed the elf. "And now, I'm going to give YOU an ear full!" he burst out hysterically, as he twisted sharply out of Wilber's grasp and left him holding a blue ear warmer! The elf hurriedly picked up his cap and raced off into the night, leaving his predecessors standing dumbfounded.

Wilber slapped his hand to his forehead in disbelief, "We were had, tricked by an elf. The first elf we ever caught and now he's no longer in our possession."

The two of them laid down silently in the soft cushion of grass for what seemed forever, relaxing and contemplating their next move but quite honestly, feeling very defeated. Finally, Wilber suddenly sat up and looked around, "Albert, the elves have all disappeared!"

Albert observed, "They've left because it's getting close to dawn, Wilber. Where did the time go anyway? Did that little Wenchneck hypnotize us or something weird?"

Albert and Wilber picked themselves up off the grass, brushing off the dew and started walking down the hill across the estate lawn. "We should've had us a truckload of elves tonight," Albert reluctantly pointed out.

"Next time, just wait, next time," Wilber vowed as he wound up his rope and opened up the gate to the sidewalk.

"Well, let's call it a night," Albert recommended. "Come on over around nine in the morning so we can make it to the circus on time, ok?"

"Later," Wilber called back, running home down the sidewalk into the early dawn underneath the streetlights.

Albert methodically climbed up a tree to the garage roof and in through his bedroom window. Finding his way over to his desk, through the dawning light, he noticed himself in the long, vertical mirror and thought to himself, "Albert is that really you?" He stared at himself staring back into near infinity. Something seemed very different with the way he felt. Very unusual, indeed.

CHAPTER FOUR

THE TRAVELING CIRCUS FROM OUTER SPACE

After a few hours of Albert rocking in his favorite chair, locked in deep contemplation, the dawn had somehow rolled into early morning. He had exhausted his writing efforts for the night and leaned back at his desk in deep satisfaction. The sun was now streaming through the bedroom window and warming up his old, aching back. Upon feeling the comforting effects, Albert began to break from his trance. He realized the morning was starting to get away and got up to loosen his rather stiff joints.

Downstairs, Martha could be heard rattling her repertoire of pans around as she prepared breakfast.

With nervous anticipation for the arrival of Wilber, Albert stepped toward the bedroom window and with his handy set of binoculars, spotted Wilber several blocks away, staring back from his bedroom window in the same manner. Reaching out the window, Albert waved at him to come over then turned and skipped out of his room.

Sliding down the bannister, as was his morning ritual, he launched himself into the kitchen where Martha sat at the table memorizing the obituaries and driving down some cold, stiff coffee. "Grits are on, Albert," muttered Martha without even losing her place in the newspaper.

"Very sorry, Martha but I've really gotta run. I'm going to the circus with Wilber and I do not want to be late for this. Care to join us?"

"Thank you so much, Albert but I don't think I can today." Martha motioned her head back and forth, directing Albert towards the door. Albert applied his 1948 derby hat to his skull and opened the door just in time to spot Wilber pushing open the white picket gate.

The two of them cleared the premises promptly, catching the good-humored Mr. Silverton on his finely manicured lawn with a butterfly net in one palm and a caged enclosure in the other. "Well, good morning, gentlemen," he puffed over his pipe. "And how was your night?" he inquired, raising his pipe back to his mouth.

"Almost had our very first Nerschvinkle Wenchneck," groaned Albert. "The elves ate very few roses though."

"Yeah, we patrolled the area very well," sustained Wilber as he and Albert stepped forward to receive their payment and a hearty thanks from Mr. Silverton.

Mr. Silverton's butler appeared from nowhere, as they often do. "Sun nectar, my dear gentlemen?" the butler offered. Everyone then (except the butler, who like all good butlers, waddled away instantly) toasted a drink and reveled over the successful patrolling of the elves last night.

"Care to accompany me to the circus now?" the zillionaire asked as he glanced at his solid gold pocket watch. He squinted exquisitely at his chauffeur who was shooting marbles with the gardener's daughter. "Warm up the limousine, Stanley. We'll be departing for the circus shortly," Mr. Silverton ordered.

The boys and Mr. Silverton made their way across his immaculate landscape to the shiny, dark green Rolls Royce. Stanley awaited and politely opened the car doors for them as the three hopped in and settled into the luxurious back seats. The Rolls hummed elegantly as they rolled down the driveway and out onto Centrifugal Drive toward the circus just a few blocks away. Mr. Silverton fiddled with the radio buttons trying to find a tune suitable to his liking.

"We interrupt this program to bring you this special bulletin. With many reports of hearing the first transmission of music from The Traveling Circus From Outer Space, we have received indications that the craft is now only a matter of miles from our planet's surface. Meanwhile, weather experts have informed us that within three minutes I repeat, within three minutes, the sound barriers will be broken. The impact on our earth's atmospheric frequencies may cause a deafening blast, followed by a severe electrical storm. Down at the fairgrounds, it is a scene of thousands of frenzied thrill seekers waiting to witness one of the most outrageous events on this side of our solar system in this century. Peter Parker here, for the Global Circuit News Agency."

The Rolls Royce was now inching slowly through the traffic outside the congested Rolling Hills Fairgrounds, eventually coasting to a halt. "Well, here we are, my friends!" Mr. Silverton proclaimed as he tapped his cane on the car window.

"Thanks Milty," offered Albert as he playfully fingered the zillionaire's curly silver locks and stepped out, watching his former college classmate hum away in his Rolls to the parking garage. Albert and Wilber moved off into the hubbub of the crowd and were swept away into the loud and buzzing turnout.

Albert and Wilber wormed their way through the nervous crowd. Outside the fairgrounds the extreme level of anticipation was suddenly snapped as the first penetration of quadrasonic music emerged through the cotton candy fog. Everyone's attention span expanded as each cranked their imaginations up toward the sky. The electronic music and grinding was becoming increasingly chilling as the craft drew nearer. In the shuffle, the overall excitement from all was frozen in unity. As babies were crying, cameramen were trying to capture this momentous arrival.

"Programs, get your programs," the one-eyed boy barked out as he turned and winked at Albert. Albert yanked one from him and strolled away to where a host of newscasters were facing cameras under intense lights.

"We can hardly even hear ourselves speak now," one of the reporters emphasized. "We're down here just outside the fairgrounds where an ecstatic crowd is taking in a most interesting display. I can now see some of the rides and the gargantuan ferris wheel is in full rotation. It's all I can do just to speak!"

Another newsman was overheard, "The colors are like none we have ever known on this planet before, extremely intense and barely even focusable. This contraption of a circus is unbelievably massive, literally out of this world."

A commentator picked up a yellow and red box and turned to the camera, "But right now, we'll take this time out for a word from one of our sponsors, brought to you by Dr. Corncob's Grits, the outspoken magician of creation. And please remember kids, one day late's too soon, so tomorrow afternoon be sure to put Dr. Corncob's on your spoon. For the Traveling Circus From Outer Space is coming to your neighborhood soon!"

The commentator caught his breath, spun around and quipped, "And the circus is also brought to you by Dr. Corncob's Fantasy Bubblegum. Blow your minds when you blow a bubble and Dr. C's face appears! Dr. Corncob's Fantasy Bubblegum comes in space-age speckled and star-tone strawberry. For school, home, work or play, chew Dr. Corncob's today!"

Albert and Wilber leaped around in uncontrollable exhilaration as they were pushed from seemingly every conceivable angle in the outcry of humanity looking up to the sky. Through the hypnotic, strobe light haze, Albert gazed up in wonderment, as in the wake of its glow, the craft commenced to lower its landing gear.

Wilber pointed up and wheeled off balance into the flooding lights and trampling crowd. The fanfare was deafening as the rides came into view, strobing at full speed. The craft hovered just above the ground now with wild, out-of-this-universe colors blinking brighter than one could ever imagine.

The lights temporarily blinded Albert as they flashed and sparked. He shielded his eyes and looked across the screaming masses and noticed that most folks had their arms up over their faces, laughing with uncertainty over this hysterical scene. The children though, were still too young to grasp what was really occurring and were running closer to the craft to watch it land. Albert had to keep running just to keep from losing sight of Wilber who was being swept away.

Albert stopped in his tracks for one last breathtaking glance as the Traveling Circus From Outer Space touched down. The nucleus of the craft then released a long hallway extension, causing another mad rush to a ticket booth located at the end. The lines were instantly very long and people were fidgeting with anticipation, leafing through their programs to plan ahead for what was in store.

Albert spotted Wilber at the very front of one of the lines. Wilber had saved him a space and the circus goers politely parted a pathway for this elderly gentleman to join young Wilber. Suddenly, things kicked into high action and the line started to move along at a very brisk pace. The center of attention now shifted to the ticket booth that was equipped with mechanical hands that handed out tickets to Albert and Wilber who snagged them quickly and stepped forward.

With one last glimpse of the world they knew behind them, they ventured down the hallway into the chaos of loud shouts, shrills and laughter as the first people rushed in. The dim hallway was lit only by small overhead runway lights. Albert was not looking ahead too much as he was captivated by the many technicolor photos of the circus performers plastered on the walls.

Albert called out to Wilber, "Come over here and look at these! Pretty wild, huh?"

But before Wilber could even react, a hair raising scream from down the hallway shook everyone to attention. They looked up to see the magician, Doctor Cornelius Corncob leaping out of a storage closet to greet the on-comers. They had to strain their necks way back to take in this massive 8 foot frame, topped off with a black and white checkered cape and cold-white flaming hair. He was a sight to behold with a very tiny, micro head attached to his gigantic shoulders and extraordinarily long, gangly arms with large baby hands. He was in fact, according to the program, only three years old, having celebrated his birthday just last week.

"Welcome earthlings," Dr. Corncob announced in a very loud and rusty voice, "to the end of the beginning, the inner universe of divine understanding. Let's bring the future home once again. Please try and find your way into the arena, for there are many secret passages to the circus from this brand new special hallway we've brought with us on this visit. And remember, obscure hope fails on the scale of intentions."

As Doctor Corncob concluded, the cameras continued to flash incessantly and newsmen hustled over the top of each other for a closer look at this spectacle, a three year old doctor of magic. He then flashed a blinding smile and ran off down the hallway waving to the hundreds of children who stampeded after their larger than life hero.

Albert and Wilber headed into the flow down the hallway where they soon came upon an intersection that divided the hallway two ways. "Which way, Albert?" Wilber motioned.

"Let's go left," Albert recommended as it was clear that no one else knew either, and besides, everyone was game for a few special surprises and new discoveries. They ventured left and found the floor to be at a slight uphill slant that wound around for another fifty feet or so until they reached a dead end and faced a revolving door.

Albert and Wilber fled through the revolving door in succession, stepping onto a circular, revolving platform that rotated them around a room filled with purple darkness. After a couple revolutions around the room and trying to contemplate how to break the secret code to exit the room, they were suddenly flooded with an arsenal of flashing strobe lights.

This wasn't just any hallway on the way to the circus, this WAS part the circus program! New panels slid into place along the walls and they now found themselves surrounded by 3D mirrors of multiple Albert's and Wilber's everywhere they turned. This was some kind of cosmic fun room!

The walls shifted again and the floor rotated Albert and Wilber around the room to an exit sign that flashed in a mirror. Albert and Wilber exchanged a quick glance and a mutual nod of agreement that this was probably the way out. They each stepped hastily through the revolving mirror and sprung out into the next hallway.

It reeked of cigars and cotton candy. Wilber broke the silence as he sniffed the odor. "We must be getting closer to the grounds, Albert. It shouldn't be too difficult for two geniuses like us to figure this out now," Wilber professed, tongue in cheek.

Albert chuckled and removed his 1948 derby hat, pushing back his hair and following Wilber who was squinting to make something out just down the hallway. By-passers appeared from all sorts of unsuspecting angles as they too found their way into the next hallway, joining Albert and Wilber in stride.

Albert pried open a thick and heavy purple velvet door and the two of them squeezed through into another room. It was a dance hall and people were moving frenetically to the space music of Marvin Mindbender and the Brainstormers, billed as "the hottest attraction from the 13th sun!"

Albert and Wilber paced quickly along the back wall, observing in awe at all the robotic, interplanetary dancing between the earthlings and the space creatures in their stunning, metallic saddle shoes. It was a very unifying experience to behold.

The sound was electrocuting and the musical notes like nothing ever heard before on earth. The faces of the band members changed constantly with the ultra pulsating rhythms and their shadows moved abstractly onto a silver and blue screen planted behind the stage. Marvin, the superior mindblower, belted out the final chorus with his 4D face making contact with all on the dance floor, elevating their senses to a new level. His fuzzy vocals resonated strongly throughout the dance hall as he finished off their number 1 hit in the western universe, "Interplanetary Chair Travel."

It was really too much to take in and almost telepathically, Albert and Wilber eyeballed the door across the dance floor and made a run for it, to escape this audio assault on their senses. As Albert and Wilber drew themselves away, the master of ceremonies pleaded loudly with the hysterical teenagers to stay down off the stage as they tried to storm Marvin Mindbender for autographs. The musicians quickly turned and fled out the backstage area to their awaiting, chauffeured space van and were urgently airlifted to their next gig.

For now, there was so much to see and to explore, that it was nerve wracking to make a decision on where to go next. Pushing through the exit, they stumbled out into the throngs of the arena fairgrounds and its spectacle of circus sounds. A two headed man was handing out rabbit balloons to all the little kids as they came in. He bellowed, "Get your balloons now while they last. Take one home and make your mother laugh!"

Albert was astounded by the brilliance of the mother ship and the shiny, platinum pipeline that protruded from the central control capsule. It took them a few breathtaking moments before Wilber caught notice of his wristwatch. "Hey Albert, it's only been three minutes since we first got into the circus!" He listened to his watch to make sure it was actually still working for it seemed like it had been a good half hour.

Just then, a universal circus usher butted in, "Well, my fine earthlings, you are now in our time zone where we know how to enjoy the fruits of life and make the time pass by ever so slowly." The usher then turned to greet the next group of patrons emerging from out of the dance hall and onto the circus fairgrounds.

By now, Albert had a pretty good idea of what to expect today and it seemed very limitless from his perspective. The footage directly in front of them was getting considerably more congested and the boys sidestepped excitedly into the mix to see what all the commotion was about.

A vendor tore off a huge chunk of rainbow cotton candy for Wilber and punched out the change on his silver belt with one of his many thumbs. Wilber snatched his treat and off he ventured with Albert leading the way, zig-zagging in and out of groupings of dazzled circus goers looking for the next big thing.

They forced their way into a gathering where next to a circus wagon, a medicine show peddler stood wagging his enormous tongue. "I am the original Bob," he proudly proclaimed. "I've got commodities of oddities and miracles in a can, universally in demand. I've had my own medicine show since half past eternity, a treasure chest full of surprises, and all at bargain prices. So step right up, if you'll please and try my homemade remedies. Superior potions, lotions and vitamins, and wholesome lives to live in."

Bob took a quick gasp of air and continued his hair-trigger diatribe, "I've got absolutely anything you need — collectibles, souvenirs and select-ables, toys, games and moonstone chains. I've got scar removers, perfumes, fragrance and scents, magical pens and chemistry sets. Folks, I've got anything you might expect, and far more than you could ever recollect. Do I have pills for aches and pains? Yes indeed, and all in this tiny bottle, my ladies. No more nagging back aches from one too many double takes."

And then Bob stepped closer to the audience for his big close. "Yes, I've got universal solutions to purify your spirit with do-it-at-home blood transfusions. Step right up, get your x-ray glasses and be the top in your classes. Take a pinch of black powder, mix it inside a can, add a bottle of liquid to complete your chemical man!"

The Original Bob sold his merchandise to the many eager spectators who lined up and clamored for his variety of pills, syrups, charms and insightful miracles.

The fanatical medicine connoisseur fired up again and sputtered, "New pathways to a longer life and shorter roads to sorrows, top of the morning tablets, and spectacular tomorrows! And now, my top shelf, secret sorceries that fulfill all the wonderful glories of life, my Eternal Happiness Potion! And isn't that all that we so deeply and so truly desire, my earthling friends?"

An old woman in a spotted dress and flowered hat clawed her way forward to the front, intensely pleading for a cure for her mediocre outlook on life.

"Then madam," negotiated Bob, "what you need is this here Eternal Happiness Potion, right here in a jar. It absolutely guarantees you miraculous contentment for years on end!" The fast talking Bob then pirouetted around and rattled on to the other onlookers with their outstretched hands as he watched the old lady rush off, crying hysterically and clutching her new potion close to her chest.

Eventually, Albert and Wilber had broken themselves away from the crowd but only after Albert had purchased a cosmic compass. Theoretically, it could read the radiation of one's brainwaves and react to any situation and help steer you into making the right decision. Albert certainly tried his best to understand this contraption. It looked very similar to an earth compass but had an electronic pulse that occasionally beat abruptly when he glared at it too long or too hard. Maybe the idea was to relax and go with the flow and just simply let the solutions come naturally, Albert concluded. With some good practice, he was sure he could get the hang of it sooner or later.

Albert hung the cosmic compass around his neck by its chain and headed toward Wilber who had been sidetracked into receiving a windmill stick from a man who was heralded as the tallest man in the universe. He posed a very striking figure over 12 feet tall and only 10 inches in diameter, so thin he nearly disappeared from view momentarily as he spun around to treat the next bunch of kids who dashed up to gawk at this most unusual creature.

His trainer pointed out to the kids and newsmen that the tallest man in the universe had no spinal cord. Men from the press clicked their cameras trying to capture the entire length of this gangly giant in their frame and began to bombard him with a smattering of questions.

"Can you swim despite the fact that you are cordless?" peppered one news reporter.

The thin man looked confused and revealed, "I guess you have not heard. I am the current high dive champion from the Space Academy and hold many records, performing dives that have never been executed by any other because of my unique physique. Next?"

Another reporter fired off "Do you find trouble finding a date on Friday nights because of your height?"

Startled by this ridiculous question, the thin man bent his extremely tall frame down so that he was now face to face with the reporter. His facial features were very leathery and grooved very deeply and his ears looked very much like a long pair of shoes. He leaned in within inches of the reporter's face and remarked, "Regarding your last question, we don't have Friday nights in outer space."

All at once, the thin man's face lit up as he surveyed overhead. With wobbling motions, he pointed up to the sky as money was raining down over the fairgrounds. An elderly man in a top hat could be seen dropping money down from an air balloon. As it drifted closer into view, Wilber cried out, "Hey, it's Mr. Silverton! Hey, Mr. Silverton, down here!" Wilber hollered, waving his hands back and forth in the air.

As onlookers whooped it up and ran around trying to pluck money out of the air, Mr. Silverton waved to the crowd and laughed in delight. The zillionaire did love to please the people. He tossed out another basket full of money and then waved goodbye to the crowd, blowing them kisses as he guided the air balloon upward and back off in the direction of his estate. The crowd absolutely loved it and bid him farewell, sending him off with a loud ovation.

Albert, who had been holding his stomach in laughter, turned as he admired his zillionaire neighbor who disappeared into the distance. But as he looked and turned in circles, it had become apparent that Wilber was gone. Albert surveyed the crowd carefully and thoroughly and spotted Wilber getting into a line and desperately motioning to him to come over and join in.

Albert scooted over in a jiffy and the two of them started to inch their way through the line, drawing closer to the monstrous main tent hosting today's feature events.

"Doctor Corncob's probably got something extra exciting up his sleeve today," Wilber forecasted. Albert nodded in agreement as they fell in stride with each other, shuffling forward and through the turnstile. Albert led the way through the dimness to where they found a pair of seats and settled back to take it all in, each breathing heavily in anticipation.

The Ringmaster of the Traveling Circus was already in progress of leading the march into the tent to massive applause and cheers. Without hesitation he skipped ahead of the cavalcade of space cadets in their starched uniforms, cracking his whip and belting out, "Good afternoon, all earthlings! We are glad we are here for you today and more than happy to come to your town. And for you out there in t.v. land, we'll be landing in your neighborhood too very soon!" The ringmaster stood in the heavy spotlight, bathing in the applause.

He then strode up to the microphone, causing a wave of ecstasy from the crowd. "Thank you, thank you so much, as he introduced with a thrilling touch, "and now - the infinite infant Dr. Corncob!!"

Doctor Corncob came on quickly with a blinding smile, transmitting a wave of nostalgia. He boasted a look of supreme concentration as he reached deeply into his vacuum of imagination. He then bowed his head, spinning rapidly toward the crowd in a circle and promptly performed his first trick, pulling a skeleton out of his skin!

The crowd quickly erupted into a deafening round of applause as there stood the one and only Doctor Cornelius Corncob, so vibrant, in full technicolor with his flaming white hair. He darted even closer to the stands and requested, "May I have a volunteer from the audience please?"

There was a loud scuffle as to the front of the stage jumped a participant who stated proudly that he went by the name of Mortimer. The crowd quickly muffled into a loud silence when Doctor Corncob took his top hat off his micro-head and placed it upside down in the center of the stage. "Climb into my hat, if you would little Mortimer."

Mortimer turned to wave at his mom and dad and all the rest in the audience before climbing on top of the hat and dropping out of sight. Everyone stared hard in utter confusion trying to figure out his trick as Dr. Corncob displayed the emptiness inside the hat. He passed the hat to a few folks in the front row and invited them to try it on and examine the hat.

Albert and Wilber nodded in approval from the 18th row in delight as the magical doctor shouted out to the mystified fans, "Mortimer is lost within the molecules amongst us all. Science will now forever be his guide." Mortimer's buddies in the front row looked on in awe, wondering and hoping they would see him again and the sooner the better so they could calm their nerves.

"Now, to make Mortimer reappear, if I could please get my hat back," Doctor Corncob requested as he reached out and gathered it in from an eager youngster and positioned the top hat carefully back onto his head.

As he stood transfixed in heavy concentration and grimacing very painfully, Doctor Corncob's hair began to flame up and his eyes grew larger and larger, starting to glow. The whole crowd was straining along with him as they too bore down and concentrated hard to bring Mortimer back. They were magnetized, staring into Doctor Corncob's laser beam eyes.

The crowd suddenly gasped in unison and shot back in their chairs in horror as a hand crawled out of Doctor Corncob's left ear. It was connected to a leg at first and then a torso followed by a contortion of limbs that slid down his leg, unraveling onto the stage, forming into a full body with its back to the audience. It then spun around to face the audience, thrusting its hands into the air. To the startled belief of all, it was a miniature Doctor Corncob!

Everyone erupted once again in a thunderous applause and then collectively held their breath as the incredible Dr. C. unzipped the side of his clone and revealed little Mortimer, who peeled off the costume and bowed to the hysterical audience. He then bolted to the safety of his parents as the house elevated its roar of approval.

Albert matched smiles and high fives with Wilber as Doctor Corncob stood at center stage, shifting his eyes back and forth with a scheming smirk. He then jumped high into the air and sunk into the floor, disappearing just like that.

The master of ceremonies rushed back onto the stage and announced, "Now my friends, at this time, we are going to pull the name of the winner of the raffle for the Star Zip Trip!! Are you ready kids?"

He then snapped his fingers and a table with a box was rolled out onto the stage as the spotlights beamed down and the music was drummed up from the Celestial Orchestra. The master continued, "The winner of the Doctor Corncob Grits box top entry will now be drawn. The question again is in so many words, tell us why you would like to tour on the Star

Zip Trip with The Traveling Circus From Outer Space and come back the day before you left?"

Albert noticed Wilber shift nervously in his seat as the gorgeous space majorette pulled an envelope from the box of entries. The drumroll intensified as she handed the winning entry to the master who revealed, "The winner of the Star Zip Trip is Newton N. Newton, the Third!! His winning answer is, "I would come back from the Star Zip Trip the day before I left, therefore enabling me to become a master of space and pass my science test on the relativity of time."

The master gave the Space Scout salute as Newton, the seven year old standout student from Nixon Elementary School, strode very proudly up to the podium to receive his Star Zip Trip Ticket. He waved to the crowd who gave him a very healthy ovation and quickly returned to his seat, showing off his prize to his friends.

The Celestial Orchestra burst into the theme song for The Traveling Circus From Outer Space, signifying that the end of the event was drawing near. The Space Cadets, and the Bearded Majorette, the cheerleaders, the fan club and the ringleader all marched around the circumference of the arena, inspiring the audience to plead for an encore.

The master of ceremonies revved up the crowd, "Let's bring Dr. C, out one more time!" He began chanting and encouraging the crowd to join in, "Dr. Corncob, Dr. Corncob, Dr. Corncob!"

Albert and Wilber were now standing on their seats, shaking their heads and clapping in unison with the rest of the fans to bring Dr. C back out to the stage. They were absolutely speechless as the good doctor suddenly appeared from behind the curtain.

The Celestial Orchestra struck up the Doctor Corncob theme song as a banner with his face was lifted up in the air and the onlookers swayed to the melody. Doctor Corncob stood in the silver spotlight, took a bow and reminded the kids, "Remember, to us from the Traveling Circus, this is outer space! Have a pleasant circus, safe travels and we'll see you kids in your dreams."

He then looked around quickly, unzipping his skin, leaving only his skeleton on stage which was then folded away into a suitcase by his shadow, who then bowed and carried the suitcase off the stage.

The master of ceremonies bounded back on stage and announced, "We must ask everyone to please disperse quickly in the next five minutes as we need to stay on schedule and lift off for another show this evening. But before you depart, everyone look under your seats! You'll be going home, the proud owner of a brand new Doctor Corncob's Dream Bubble, his new invention that records your dreams, play by play. Set it by your bed by night. Awake in the morning and watch your dreams on a close circuit screen. And of course, it's pocket sized and solar energized!"

The master continued, "Newton N. Newton, you are requested to report immediately to the main capsule for your Star Zip Trip that will be departing in exactly three minutes and counting! And as a special surprise, you can bring your two friends, Albert and Wilber who were the runners up. They will get to join you on the first leg of the trip as we crack through the ozone."

Newton grabbed Albert and Wilber who were stunned in disbelief. None of them were ready for the gravity and immediacy of the situation. They grabbed each other and jumped up and down in excitement.

Newton expressed his concern, "I need to go ask my parents real quickly if it's ok to go!"

"Newton," Wilber reminded Newton, "Have you forgotten that you are getting back the day before you left?! Therefore, you don't need to worry in the least bit about getting permission." Wilber winked at Albert who was having the same epiphany.

Newton scratched his beanie and laughed, "Oh yeah, I just can't get my mind wrapped around the concept."

Albert nudged Newton and Wilber toward the craft and urged them to snap out of it and carry on with the mission. The three of them turned toward the spaceship, breathed in a deep dose of courage and marched forth as other circus patrons rushed out in the opposite direction.

The Captain spotted the three and cracked the door to the main capsule, hastily motioning them in. "Boys, hustle up now! We will be departing in ninety seconds. Newton, nice to meet you. You may take a seat right here between me and the co-captain. Albert and Wilber, come with me upstairs." They obeyed and followed the Captain up a spiral staircase to a second capsule.

"Now listen up closely. Strap yourself into these two seats right away. We will be lifting off in sixty seconds. Just relax and enjoy the view. Don't be alarmed if you see a few other spaceships along the way. You must know, they are always out there but through our special 4D glass, you will be able to easily spot them in the parallel dimension, like the flip side of a coin. It's just that you earthlings can only see in 3D and wouldn't normally see them. This is for your own good and sanity," he winked.

"You'll get to ride along with us on this flight for only about ten minutes and then we will launch your capsule. You will land safely just a few minutes later in a very magical place we are certain you will enjoy, courtesy of the Star Zip Trip and The Traveling Circus From Outer Space. Good luck, gentlemen."

The Captain tipped his hat and scurried back down the spiral staircase to the main controls. Albert and Wilber strapped in tightly, clutching their hands nervously and got prepared to blast off. They secured their space helmets and oxygen masks and gave each other their usual nod of assurance as they had all their lives, as best friends do.

Albert's thoughts were soon scrambled in an intense vibration and sudden jerk as he was thrust back into his seat. The circus machinery was grinding furiously and before Albert or Wilber could even react, The Traveling Circus From Outer Space lifted off with a magnificent force, propelling into the clouds.

The boys looked down and could briefly see the townspeople and circus goers, waving goodbye, shielding their eyes from the glare and heat of the explosive lift-off. Albert spotted his house, and Mr. Silverton's and then Wilber's too before the school and factories became tiny geometric shapes in the distance.

As the craft increased its speed and power, soon even the rivers, lakes and farm fields began to look minuscule and the majestic mountains outside of town were reduced to just small hills of rubble and snow caps. Albert and Wilber leaned forward in their seats to crane their head closer to the window as they watched their town in the evening sunset vanish from view over the next few seconds.

This was a far different experience than any jet they had ever flown on. As they shot higher and higher into the sky, it wasn't long before they were able to see not only their state but a vast expanse of the whole country and its bright, blue waters.

Soon, the feeling of the thrust and G-force had subsided and it seemed like they were just more or less floating gently toward space and feeling light as a feather. As Albert gazed upward through the skylight, he was amazed how clear the stars and planets were and felt like he could almost reach out and grab a beam. It was at this moment that Albert also recognized that there seemed to be a very faint thread of light between all the stars as if they were all networked or hooked together in some kind of an intricate pattern.

"Wilber, are you seeing what I'm seeing? Everything is interconnected."

Wilber marveled for a moment, "Almost like we're inside a molecular structure, isn't it, Albert?"

"Could be that maybe our universe that we think we know so well is nothing more than a singular molecule," contemplated Albert.

"Humbling," admitted Wilber. "Very humbling."

The two of them settled back into a reclining position with their hands behind their heads and for the next few minutes, not a word was exchanged as they soaked in this very special moment, gliding effortlessly toward the stars.

They were suddenly shaken out of their trance by a hostess who had made her way up to their capsule. "Good afternoon, Albert and Wilber. I'm afraid you'll need to be exiting the craft in half a minute."

She held out a tray and offered them each a beverage. "Here, wash this juice down quickly. It will help you adjust to the sudden drop in altitude you will be experiencing and allow you to comfortably fall into a deep sleep as you re-enter the atmosphere."

The boys happily obliged and gulped down the juice in a matter of seconds.

The hostess instructed them, "Now, in just 15 seconds and counting, push this orange Launch button very firmly and your capsule will dislodge from the main craft. Your capsule will safely navigate back down to earth and is programmed to land in a lagoon just off the Hardwood Forest where we hope you will enjoy continuing your journey."

She added, "You don't need to do a thing but relax and enjoy. After you land and float to the shore, simply exit the capsule and the Captain will send for it to rejoin us in space. On behalf of The Traveling Circus From Outer Space, good day and we hope you had the flight of a lifetime."

She then quickly departed and as the buzzer sounded loudly, Wilber took the honor of pounding hard on the orange launch button. They were immediately catapulted away from the main craft and headed downward.

Albert and Wilber gazed up and watched the ominous Traveling Circus contraption and its giant, blinking ferris wheel, lumber off into space toward the next lucky planet. The kids there would absolutely love the show and were in for quite a treat. Albert wondered if Newton would be fortunate enough to be their guest.

The capsule began to pick up tremendous speed and overwhelming G-force as it hurtled toward earth. Albert and Wilber tightened their seat belts, each taking a huge breath of anxiety and closing their eyes tightly, preparing themselves for a splash landing that could come any minute. Their eyelids felt heavier and heavier as they rapidly slipped away into a peaceful slumber.

CHAPTER FIVE

THE HARDWOOD FOREST

The sun was just beginning to poke its head over the foggy horizon of the lavender lagoon as Albert's eyes were gently massaged by the first glimmer of morning sunbeams. He rubbed his eyes as he struggled to recognize his whereabouts and the strange events of yesterday. Looking around in the capsule, it all started coming back to Albert as he noticed Wilber beginning to stir from his sleep.

Peering out the window, Albert squinted to make out the images through the drifting fog. Their capsule was floating in a lagoon containing beautiful lavender water and heading toward the shore, not too far in the distance. A soft breeze kept nudging them closer.

"Wilber!" Albert whispered loudly, being careful not to frighten him. "Time to shake it."

As Wilber came to, Albert outlined that they had evidently landed overnight in a lagoon and were about to hit the shore. Wilber cupped his hands around his eyes and leaned forward, seeing what he could discover out his window. From his vantage point, he spotted a gaggle of pink flamingos fishing for their breakfast just off the shore. Nearby, three clown children knelt in the sand at the water's edge, sailing paper ships with their checkered hands. The parent clowns were just a few feet to the left, pondering their reflection in the water as they refreshed their makeup.

The serenity of the smooth, glass-like water was suddenly broken as a gigantic, 1914 rainbow trout lunged out of the water, snagging a fly in mid-air before splashing back into the depths of the lagoon.

"Hey, where do you suppose we are, exactly, Wilber?" questioned Albert as he squinted out his window.

Wilber responded, "Remember, the captain said something about dropping us off at the Hardwood Forest and that we might find ourselves in a parallel universe?"

"Hey, that's right," Albert recalled. "It's part of the runner up prize for the Star Zip Trip. I think Dr. Corncob has given us a challenging assignment for finding our way back home, Wilber. And if you think about it, I've had a little experience with that very recently. I think I'm sort of getting the hang of it. We might not be all that far away from home, you know? In fact, it might be just beyond our fingertips."

"I do not disagree," confirmed Wilber as he pushed his glasses up, "and I do hereby accept the challenge."

Just then, the boys felt a little jolt as the capsule bottomed out on the shoreline. "Hey, we've hit the shore! Let's blow this popsicle stand!" Albert instructed with a wink. They both quickly unbuckled their safety harnesses and removed their helmets. Albert took in a deep breath to give him extra strength and wrestled with the latch to the exit door, giving it all his effort and forcing it open.

A batch of fresh air hit the two of them as they stretched their limbs and climbed out of the capsule and into a foot of warm, bath-like water. It felt so good to finally be able to stand straight up and breathe in the morning air. It smelled like that of sweet jasmine.

The clown family quietly slinked away into the shadows, unsure of these earthlings, even though they seemed to be rather friendly and harmless. As Albert surveyed the area, they were standing at the edge of a forest and as he looked more closely, a trail made of hardwood flooring ended where the shoreline met the forest.

Off to the right of the floor a bit, Wilber spotted two grandfather geniuses playing checkers in the shade, intensely speculating further moves, while sipping diligently on their lemonade.

"Wait here, Wilber," Albert whispered as he wandered over to the beginning of the Hardwood Floor and followed it up a few feet to where the checker game was in progress.

"Hello, hello, gentlemen," Albert announced. "My name is Albert and over there is my associate, Wilber. I would like to ask you about matters pertaining to using a telephone, if I may."

But neither genius noticed him, being that they were so mesmerized by their game and studying the mental combat on the checker board. The genius on the right moved one of his red checkers forward and smiled slyly at his opponent.

"A very excellent move," the genius on the left commented as he pointed to a stooped over figure just a ways down the Hardwood Floor. "See the Old Wise Lady of the Forest, Albert. She will take your journey under advisement."

"Thank you kindly," offered Albert as he motioned for Wilber to join him at the head of the Hardwood Floor. They proceeded rather cautiously down the floor a ways towards this very short and hunched over elderly woman. She had a long, skinny nose and waist-long grey hair streaming down her back.

She peered up at them from her hunched over position and crackled, "So may I assume you will be journeying down the Hardwood Floor and you want to know how in the world to get home?"

"Yes ma'am," Wilber answered rather sheepishly.

She pointed down the floor with her cane clutched in her furry palms, "Homeward will lay just beyond the forest." She then paused as she straightened up and inched in very closely to Albert and Wilber, locking her eyes intently with theirs.

Albert and Wilber felt a chill tighten up their necks as she spoke through a pipe hanging from her ancient lips. "To find your way home, you must lift your heart ever so gently and listen very openly to all that surrounds you. Quiet your mind and the answers will come to you so easily and guide you safely home."

The boys stood very quietly, absorbing her words of wisdom as they watched the Old Wise Lady of the Forest turn away and then disappear into the black forest that she had probably walked time and time again over the past few centuries.

Meanwhile, Albert was finally recognized by one of the clown children named Benny, whose eyes lit up as he waved, kneeling in the crystal sand. Albert winked back and wheeled around to catch the backside of Wilber who was heading down the Hardwood Floor. Taking one last scan, Albert made his way onward, observing as much as possible along the way so he could keep his bearings. The forest was very thick here on both sides and if one wandered off the floor very far, it would seem relatively certain, that he could get lost.

Ahead of him, Wilber had stopped cautiously with a look of astonishment and his hand up, signaling Albert to stop. "Be very still, Albert," Wilber hushed. "Look through that clearing," he directed ahead.

Circling through the underbrush of the forest, was the Clown Army sneaking toward a wizard who was innocently sleeping under a tree with his fortune of jewels hidden under his hat on the ground beside him. He began to snore heavily and twitch as one does when they are in such a deep slumber.

The Clown Army crawled army style, inching closer to the wizard, as all the squirrels and little animals scattered in a frantic chatter. The bandit clowns in their size 24 shoes, slipped about the trees, when suddenly the wizard popped up from his snooze, sending the clowns into a freeze!

The wizard looked around suspiciously before closing his weakened eyes to resume his rest. One of the clowns, believed to be the Captain, crept forward and knelt before the old wizard. Albert and Wilber listened in from their crouched position behind a bush.

The captain whispered quietly into the wizard's ear in hypnotizing fashion, "Fall backwards into a sleep. You are going back, back, back in time as you follow the years away into the distance of your childhood. The past will reveal your dreams in thousands of word paintings and the silence will carry you down stream to where the memories of your treasures lay."

"Now, tell us where your treasures are hidden, Mr. Wizard," the head clown impatiently grilled, as the vigilante clown army crept mechanically forward, trying to keep from tripping over their ridiculously oversized shoes.

But the whereabouts would never be told as a stampede of yellow, velvet horses thundered down the Hardwood Floor, quickly closing in on the scene, sending the Clown Army diving into the underbrush for cover. The horses galloped gallantly down the Hardwood Floor with their red manes of silk blowing back in the wind as they made their way down to the lagoon to quench their thirst.

The Clown Army decided to quickly change their plan and flopped away toward the lagoon to spy on the horses and see if they could catch one or two for their infantry back at their base camp.

Meanwhile, Albert and Wilber slipped out of the bushes and cautiously continued down the Hardwood Floor away from the pandemonium. It wasn't too long down the floor before they settled into a sense of deep peace, listening to the sounds made by unknown animals of rarity heard over a stream's constant rush over the rocks. Overhanging willows cast shadows of pink as they rounded a curve and came upon a small clearing and secluded park.

The air here was very motionless and Wilber was showing signs of uncertainty but Albert took the whole thing very optimistically. "Wilber, the bright pink shadows are actually a very positive sign, I believe. For if this area were truly dangerous, do you not think the shadows would be black and not pink?"

Wilber pondered momentarily before admitting that Albert's shadow theory was in pretty good judgment. Wilber began to whistle. After all, he did love to whistle and it did seem to work in calming him down.

At an opening in the trees, both had decided to slow their pace and find some quality time in the sun, enjoying the warm sunshine that soothed their foreheads.

They came to a halt as they detected a strange, humanly mumble around the next bend in the floor. Curiosity began to unfold as both edged their way forward far enough to see a rather old and fashionably dressed Fabler in a floppy red beret sitting on a park bench. He was reading in a shallow voice to a somewhat distorted looking boy who was surrounded by many, many birds.

The Fabler caught a glimpse of Albert and Wilber peering from around the bend. "Come on over, gentlemen and sit around. We are about to embark on a new story, I'm sure you'll enjoy!" He chuckled aloud and seemed to be a very jovial and trusting soul.

Albert and Wilber trudged out of the bushes and toward the bench, sitting opposite of the distorted boy. The Fabler introduced them to this strange looking child with the horse-like face. "My friends, this is one of my most frequent customers. He is Edgar and this is his collection of birds. And what might the two of you be named?"

"Name's Albert. How's it doing? By the way, do you know where a telephone might be found?"

"No, no, I sure don't think you'll find any here in The Hardwood Forest" the Fabler winked, shaking his curly locks back and forth.

"And I'm Wilber, sir. We went to The Traveling Circus From Outer Space yesterday and got second place in the Star Zip Trip. We landed here in the lagoon this morning and I'm quite certain that my parents would sure appreciate a call. They're most likely very concerned that we didn't come home last night even though it is the day before we left."

"Well, Albert and Wilber," the Fabler carefully considered, "there are no telephones here, let me assure you. But if you dare, Eastern Paranoia should have many. Just stay on your journey and follow the Hardwood Floor deeper and deeper into the forest. You'll figure it out, I assure you. As a matter of fact, Edgar can lead you down the floor a ways. He needs to return home to the Genius Colony anyway and he can sure use the company. Edgar, please show them the way, if you would and we'll see you for another reading tomorrow, ok?"

Over and around the bend, the two of them followed Edgar's lead up the hillside turning slightly to the left at a very brisk pace. Edgar croaked out in short sentence fragments about something he had just found in the forest. He was trying to explain in a broken speech pattern that he had discovered a box while scanning the ground for birds and that this special box contained the answer he had been searching for to take back to the Genius Colony.

No longer had Wilber tried to make out Edgar's logic when there was an elderly, raspy voice calling out from down the Hardwood Floor, beckoning for Edgar to come home.

"Grandfather Genius is calling for me. I better go now," Edgar murmured to the trailing Albert and Wilber. "Coming Grandfather, coming," Edgar echoed up the path.

Up ahead was an indentation in the trees where a circle of tall wooden partitions surrounded the opening. Grandfather Genius was perched upright in his favorite chair, with his humongous head bulging at the collar of his gown. He eyed Edgar and his guests carefully. "Please be seated, Edgar. And who is it that you have brought back with you on your adventures today?"

All eyes from the members of the Genius Colony were fixated on the two strangers standing in the back shadows. Albert stepped out into the light. "Albert, here," he pronounced. "And this, my friends, is Wilber."

Grandfather Genius acknowledged, "Your presence is welcome here in the Genius Colony. Please come unto me now. I have something for the two of you if you would now come forward."

As Albert and Wilber drew closer toward him, Grandfather Genius reached into a pocket of his purple robe and pulled out two beautiful necklaces of mirror stone. Only feet away now, the boys could feel the friendliness of his eyes embracing them. His very prominent wrinkles displayed many, many valleys of deep wisdom. Albert and Wilber now stood before him as the rest of the colony encircled them and held hands.

Grandfather reached over and placed a necklace over Albert's head and likewise on Wilber. "I am eye," Grandfather Genius chanted, bowing graciously. "I am eye."

The congregation echoed back, flashing their mirror necklaces with sun reflections back into Albert and Wilber's eyes, "I am eye. I am eye."

An understudy by the name of Alexander The Magnificent then presented Albert and Wilber with a Drink of the Frozen Tide People. "Step this way please," he softly commanded. "Follow me and allow me to propose a toast."

They were led to where Edgar had been positioned in a tall, metal chair. Wires from an IQ meter were strapped to his head and dangled awkwardly all the way down to his feet.

Alexander pulled Albert and Wilber close to his side, while removing his glass eye and clued them in. He whispered softly to them, "You must know that Edgar has reached the age of verdict. We are running a series of IQ tests to see if Edgar is still a genius. If not, I'm afraid he cannot possibly remain in our Genius Colony any longer, for obvious reasons."

As the colony of geniuses in their satin purple gowns closed in, surrounding Edgar in a circle, they all clasped hands and began to hum as Alexander raised a huge flask high above his head containing the Drink of the Frozen Tide People. "To Edgar, who today, has come of age. May his wisdom forever flourish and shine as bright as the sun!"

The colony chanted, "To Edgar!" as Alexander took a huge swig from the flask and passed it on to the next genius. Grandfather Genius pulled hard on the lever of the IQ meter strapped to Edgar's head. The contraption began to vibrate and spark as the needles on the meters swung wildly back and forth. As each genius took a swig from the Drink of the Frozen Tide People, they began to hum louder as their huge temples pulsated in rhythm to the buzzing of the wires that protruded from Edgar's head.

Albert nudged Wilber who was locked in concentration with the pulsation of the chanting ritual. He wished with all his might for the success of their new found friend of the forest.

Albert could practically feel the currents shooting through Edgar's brain as his eyes lit up and his hair stood on end. The genius colony began to chant even louder as they each approached Edgar, shining the sun's rays from their mirror necklaces into Edgar's eyes.

Once each member had made the pilgrimage to Edgar's chair, Grandfather Genius rose from his throne and walked gracefully toward the center of the circle. He raised his arms upward toward the sky while the colony quieted down quickly, now nervously awaiting the results. Grandfather Genius shuffled toward Edgar and carefully examined all the readings and meters attached to his head. He stroked his century old beard as he grumbled softly, calculating all the readings.

The silence grew even louder as Grandfather Genius gently removed the wires from Edgar and proclaimed, "My grandson Edgar, I'm afraid you are not a genius anymore."

Grandfather Genius stood before the congregation, slightly slumped over with heavy eyes and continued, "Edgar, according to the test, you seem to have lost the key to your inner vision, depth and sight."

Edgar just sat back, frozen in his seat as his pale face registered a look of shock.

Grandfather Genius put his arm around Edgar and advised him, "You must be off now in search of the Old Wise Lady of the Forest. For only she can reignite your wisdom, help you discover your highest intentions for living and restore your laughter that's been missing. Be it unto yourself to now be taken by her guiding hand and brought through The School of Wisdom & Light."

"Go there to embrace her teachings and gather all the enlightenment that is ever so abundant. It's highly regarded as a sacred place, where birds of space constantly chime in nursery rhyme. Go forth now to the School of Wisdom & Light—it's just beyond the Bridge of 5 Miles High."

Edgar suddenly jumped down from his chair, stumbled for a moment and ran off down the Hardwood Floor toward the bridge. Grandfather Genius stooped over in hopeless concern. "He's a good boy, that Edgar. I wish for him the best of luck and a brilliant return to prominence. Yes, indeed. The Old Wise Lady of the Forest is our only hope now that remains."

He then penetrated deeply into the eyes of Albert. "And what is it that you are in search of Albert? Is it she too that you must find?"

"Not exactly," Albert responded. "But we have seen her earlier today."

"Yeah," Wilber piped in, "back at the lagoon."

Grandfather Genius widened his eyes in surprise. "She has traveled very far in her old age. I hope she returns to the School of Wisdom & Light before Edgar's arrival there. I have sent a messenger to inform her of his arrival. Perhaps she has come to visit us for more sessions or maybe she is hunting for mushrooms. Tell me boys, did she carry a basket?"

Albert rolled back his memory. "As a matter of fact, I believe she did, come to think of it."

"Fine, fine. That means she will be returning home soon," Grandfather Genius reflected. "Ok, gentlemen. If you see her, please let her know of Edgar's condition. If she is near, I would like to request her presence very soon."

"Yes sir," Albert agreed as he estimated their assignment. After all, he thought they were headed the opposite way from this morning and perhaps they would see her when they got to the Bridge of 5 Miles High.

Grandfather Genius then smiled ever so warmly with his forehead swelling in delight. "Thank you, Albert and Wilber. Now where is it that the both of you are headed?"

"We're still looking for a telephone booth in some place called Eastern Paranoia," Albert answered.

Wilber added, "We're from Centrifugal Drive in Suburbia Heights. Ever hear of it?"

"Oh yes of course, of course I have. I do believe I recall hearing about it maybe 70 years ago," Grandfather Genius estimated. "It's in a parallel universe just outside the Subway to the Inner Fields of Self Identity. So near, yet so much farther than our comprehension can possibly stretch. Yet, still very attainable when one is highly focused and seeing beyond the truth."

"Parallel universe?" Wilber questioned. That's the second time in two days we have heard that. "Is it like turning a molecule inside out or something?"

"Yes, something like that, son. It deals more with the proper balance of nature. I'm sure you'll find the enlightenment as soon as you discover or develop another sensory within you. But until that time, the only way out is on the Subway to the Inner Fields of Self Identity. Telephones are of no help to you at this point. You must call upon yourself for proper guidance homeward, not a telephone. I regret to inform you that the only entrance to the Subway that we know of is in Eastern Paranoia. I presume that you have been warned of its existence?"

"We'll be very mindful," Albert assured.

"No doubt, you will." Grandfather Genius chuckled with a glint in his eyes. "Well good luck to the two of you. Your journey will be very beautiful at first but it will also pose much danger."

He then reached to his side into a treasure box and pulled out two flasks, extending them out in his ancient hands. "Here, Albert. And this one is for you, Wilber. This is the Drink of the Frozen Tide People. Drink from this when you need encouragement and light." He then bowed, "Farewell then."

"I am eye," Albert winked graciously.

Inspired, the boys turned gratefully and headed up the Hardwood Floor. Step by step, they walked deeper into thoughts of wonder. Consistently, they maintained a hurried pace, even though it was rather peaceful here as the midday sunshine revealed its light, sliding between the trees.

For the first few minutes, Edgar's frustrated babbling could be heard in the distance, as the wind carried it from somewhere up ahead in the deep regions of the forest.

"Kind of hope we get to see Edgar again," sounded Wilber, kicking along with his hands in his pockets. "It's not really his fault that he's not a genius anymore."

"No kidding," Albert agreed, still gripped in the aftermath.

As they headed off, a film of wind lightly swept across their new memories as they sidewinded up the Hardwood Floor. After they had journeyed on for nearly three long hours into the mid afternoon, they ducked under overhanging branches that shadowed the floor and came upon a clearing where it was sunny once again. Their eyes were enriched by very brightly illuminated gardens on both sides of the floor.

Clusters of exploring seekers were roving through the Dimensional Gardens, quietly chattering away, sharing their discoveries with each other.

Above a grove of giant orange sunflowers, exotic yellow birds flashed throughout the sky, darting in and out of the gardens. They provided a spectacular aerial ballet as they flew in unison, edging through the hedging, veering near the shearing, and zipping past the clippings. A gardener's ever-so-happy whistle could be heard through the thistle as she worked like mad to clip away the bad. She gathered as many precious satin petals of church flowers as she possibly could manage and scooped them into her basket as she hummed to the sky for sweet showers to come.

Light musical strains approaching from further up the Hardwood Floor lured the two boys away and off they went. Up ahead, a small boy stood at the feet of an organ grinder. As the two noticed Albert and Wilber heading up the floor toward them, the organ grinder started to crank away more loudly on his box and the boy smiled broadly to get their attention as he jumped up and down with a sign.

You are cordially invited to a bout of
Championship Croquet
The Monkeys versus The Children of the Forest
at 3:00 sharp today

The organ grinder beckoned for those who wanted to come, to follow him as he churned his handle rhythmically and dashed up the Hardwood Floor to a place called Accordion Meadows. There stood an exquisite croquet course lined with adoring fans and royalty who had come from afar to place their bets on this championship match.

Two speckled anteaters moved about, grazing on dandelions, removing the obstacles from the field of play. The head groundskeeper of the Accordion Meadows inspected the course closely as the master of ceremonies climbed the tower up to his platform chair where he would oversee the proceedings. The patrolman with a rabbit face and a night stick slapping in his hand, chewed his gum professionally, telling the fans where to stand.

On the practice field to the right, The Monkeys could be seen working out as the organ grinder led the pursuers into the crowd. The star Monkey croquet player in his tightly fitted derby hat stared in cold precision as he executed a perfect putt between the wicket. He then whipped around and shot a smug grin in the direction of The Children's captain. The tension was mounting and the crowd began to murmur in anticipation as the clock wound down to the start of the match.

Leading their forces, the Monkeys began to chatter it up very loudly as they loped to center course to meet the awaiting Children of the Forest. They stared each other down, eye to eye.

At precisely 3pm, the buzzer sounds
Necks craning from out of bounds
Eyes leaning to the center green
For the announcement of the starting team

Albert whistled nervously and pleaded with Wilber, "I'd love to stay and watch but we really need to get going before it gets dark and we're maybe only an hour or so away now from the bridge."

Albert and Wilber slipped away and shuffled briskly up the Hardwood Floor, once again setting their sights on the Bridge of 5 Miles High, so close now they could almost feel it.

After another hour, hunger had begun to take full effect on their hollow stomachs and they stopped to snatch a couple handfuls of blueberries and rest. The Hardwood Floor had begun to rise in elevation and was testing their strength after being on their feet a greater part of the day. And after all, Albert was seventy-seven years old and beginning to slow down. Wilber understood this and studied Albert carefully to make sure he was doing alright. He had noticed that something was not quite normal with Albert. And had Albert actually gone to sleep last night?

Nevertheless, the boys embarked again and trudged uphill for another mile, battling a very stiff headwind and coming to a sudden halt after coming to the crest of a hill.

There it was! Before them was The Bridge of 5 Miles High, a monstrous structure that extended high into the clouds. At the foot of the bridge, sat a strange silhouette propped in a chair.

"And now?" Albert gasped as he and Wilber awaited, catching their breath and holding back behind an overarching tree branch.

"Let's go for it," recommended Wilber. "We haven't any other choice. He's already seen us anyhow. I'll bet he's a nice enough of a man."

"Ok then," Albert concluded, "let's do this."

The two slipped out nonchalantly from under the branch and tackled the curvature up the remainder of the Hardwood Floor, obviously acting undisturbed and carefree. They made their way the last fifty feet to the foot of the bridge.

Each was immediately greeted by a stern looking Bridge Attendant sitting stiffly in his high backed chair. His heart could visibly be seen ticking inside a glass chamber wall of his chest. He held up his stop sign and greeted them, "Welcome to The Bridge of 5 Miles High! To make certain of your safety, you'll be required to fit on a pair of suction cup shoes."

Wilber, who was feeling more than a little tad bit nervous, blurted out, "Do you mind if we have a rest and some drink?"

"Very well," the Bridge Attendant replied with his whip eyelashes whistling in the wind.

Each pulled their flasks from their belts and guzzled with haste from The Drink of the Frozen Tide People. Grandfather Genius had been so generous in providing them this gift of divine nourishment. It filled them with inspiration for this challenging escapade about to take place across the Bridge of 5 Miles High. With a final gulp of drink and two gulps of caution, they put the caps back on and looked to the Bridge Attendant for the go-ahead to proceed.

Reaching into his old burlap sack, the Bridge Attendant presented them both with sun visor caps with bills so long one could almost look up inside the sky. Then without hesitation, Albert and Wilber fit snuggly into their suction cup shoes and practiced a few steps up the beginning of the bridge.

"A long journey is within you," the attendant offered, following along with them the first few steps to make sure they were safe and steady. He then sported a childish grin and looked down at his watch. "Please hurry, there isn't much light left. Before dark, you must make the bridge's end. And please, try not to daydream or freeze in ease or seize a nap in the breeze" he chuckled. "And do say hello to my twin brother at the opposite end."

The last goodbye was exchanged as Albert and Wilber gazed longingly out over the valley of mountain strands caressing the sky. A bank of orange and pink clouds surrounded the bridge further up ahead near the highest part. It was all they could do to not dare look down into miles and miles of a seemingly bottomless canyon.

More scaling of the bridge loomed ahead. The incline was thankfully gradual and as Albert and Wilber hiked their way into the cloudy ceiling, their visibility had been reduced to less than twenty or thirty feet. Therefore, they took extra measures to make their footing very precise.

As they squinted hard to scout what was on the bridge ahead, an odd figure could be faintly seen coming into the picture now out of the cloudy splotches riding a unicycle.

High on the bridge
Way into the clouds
See Oliver on a unicycle
Weaving carelessly around

Searching for the old lady
The one so kind and wise
He knows she holds the key
To the dreams he's left behind

He doesn't know where he is
And doesn't care besides
Oliver spends all of his days
On the unicycle he rides

He only smiles with dimly shut eyes
Happy as he could be
Life doesn't get him down
It's only what you see

Away rides Oliver all over the bridge
Never once losing his smile
For this is his pleasurable moment
On the Bridge of 5 Miles High

Oliver wobbled by, leaving Albert and Wilber harmoniously shouting navigations at him until he had zig-zagged his way into a cumulus mass and was soon out of sight.

Albert and Wilber both breathed a sign of relief and continued onward for several minutes, finally reaching the top of the bridge. They stopped on the plateau to catch their wind and to refresh their dry mouths with more of that glorious Drink of the Frozen Tide People. The clouds had drifted apart, making way for a stream of early yellow sunset that warmed their skin. Everything seemed very tranquil and peaceful again as the late afternoon gave way to evening.

Suddenly without notice, a very long bird, specifically known as a mammoth raven, consisting of a thirty-eight foot wing span, glided under the bridge directly under the boys. It must have been the size of a school bus. It belted out a horrendous and ancient squawk that echoed off the canyon walls so loudly that Albert had to cover his ears. The creature was a thing of beauty as it quickly swooshed through the canyon and off into the distant horizon.

Albert and Wilber both cracked up in awe at this sight and slowly clumped away as hard as possible through the thick clouds listening to the bird's screeches, still piercing back off the canyon ridges. The bird then took a hard bank to the right and circled back with an arsenal of aerial dynamics, offering only a faint, white blur as it flipped gracefully and majestically, soaring upside down. Absolute poetry in motion.

With the peak of the bridge behind them now, they paced themselves steadily as they started dipping into a valley of the floor. The footing here was more tricky heading downhill and after a few hundred yards, the boys got the hang of it, feeling a calming sense of relief to be finally heading down to a lower elevation.

Albert glared into the short horizon with his mind scanning what appeared to be a rest stop area on a much wider section of the bridge that flattened outward. There was a sweet smell of food in the air and as they drew closer they could make out picnic tables that were set for dinner. Time seemed to stand still here and the wind had died down to a very gentle breeze, just enough to cool them off a little bit as they approached.

A kitchen maid pushing a dinner cart of hot, steaming dumplings came clumping toward them from out of the fog. She stopped just short of the boys and curtsied in the soft coated wind, suggesting a table for two in a little fog clearing.

As much as their tummies desired a nice warm meal, Albert and Wilber politely declined and waved goodbye to her as they needed to make their destination and set out again. Vapors were rising all about them as they made their way toward the proximity of a mountain ledge. Here, the land welcomed the floor onto its strand of crystal that rose from the depths of fog. Albert tightened his smile and could feel his heart racing and his spirits rising. It wouldn't be too much longer now before they would reach the end of the bridge and once again feel safe to be back on solid ground.

Without a word uttered, Albert and Wilber challenged the pace they had set and hurried toward the end of the bridge. Wilber, who had the much sharper eyes, became curious about a sign that pointed down the final straightaway of the bridge to where a silhouette sat upright in a spindle chair.

No chance could be risked at such a thing as this by moving a little too fast or even too slowly for that matter. The trick would be to approach rather nonchalantly, perhaps even whistle a little bit and pretend to be passing by like any other ordinary day.

With their game plan on, Albert and Wilber stepped off the final twenty or thirty steps and pulled up alongside the seated silhouette. Wilber took a gulp and walked around the chair to have a peek and declared, "Albert, you won't believe this but it's the Bridge Attendant's twin brother! He wasn't kidding."

"No big deal," the Bridge Attendant shrugged as he unwound his yo yo off the cliff on a string so long, it nearly touched the valley of clouds below. He then straightened his posture and repositioned himself to speak to the boys more directly. "You should exit the bridge right away before we close it for the evening. Just follow this path off the end of the bridge to the right and follow it down the mountain side for a quarter mile. You'll see the signs if it hasn't grown too dark, that is."

Albert and Wilber sat down on a bench next to the Bridge Attendant and removed their suction cup shoes. They waved goodbye, bid him a generous thank you and worked their way to the end of the bridge.

When they were out of ear shot, Wilber whispered, "Is that for real—the bridge attendant's twin? Must have something to do with striking the perfect balance or something, like yin and yang."

At the foot of the bridge, they stepped off, took a hard right and bounded down a steep trail. They were so grateful to once again be setting foot on the sweet soil of this earth. They laughed uncontrollably as they hustled breathlessly down the hillside, weaving their way through caves hung on mountain ledges, navigating down glass rock staircases and through underpasses of ancient trees.

At last, after a quarter mile, the land flattened out a bit on a plateau as they stumbled upon a crossroad of more hardwood floors. A sign pointed to the right for The School of Wisdom and Light. They made their way down the Hardwood Floor toward a beautiful waterfall that seemed to pour majestically out of the sky.

Passing over a small footbridge behind the waterfall, Albert and Wilber took a moment to stop and look up and take it all in. It felt so refreshing to get a little soaked and cool off as they had both worked up quite a sweat in their excitement. Through the roaring of the water, they could make out some voices up ahead.

As they snuck quietly up the floor they came upon a glen of fruit trees, where yes indeed, the Old Wise Lady of the Forest stood in the middle of a circle of forest children. They all had their text books open and were following along by candlelight to her instructions.

Not wanting to interrupt the Old Wise Lady and her flock of ragamuffins, Albert tugged at Wilber to come along. But their eyes met hers and they nodded in a secret understanding. Albert noted quietly to Wilber that Edgar was in attendance. Mission accomplished. For Edgar was now safe and sound.

The Old Wise Lady motioned for them to stop and she excused herself from the students for a moment to make her way out to see Albert and Wilber. She asked of them, "In the interest of my heart, where will you boys be staying tonight?"

"Home if possible," began Albert slowly. "If only we knew exactly how to get there."

"I'm afraid that Eastern Paranoia is the only option for you," the Old Wise Lady claimed acidly. "Now, let me offer you some advice. Look for my sister there and she will help you. Please, please do as I recommend for I must now go back to my little ones as the sun is going down very, very soon and I'm about to lose power."

"You can catch a trolley to Eastern Paranoia just down the Hardwood Floor a ways, right behind the very last apple tree you come to. But you best hurry along. The last trolley of the evening will be arriving in about two minutes. Nice to see you again, gentlemen and I do hope you have thoroughly enjoyed your day in the Hardwood Forest."

CHAPTER SIX

EASTERN PARANOIA

Albert and Wilber waved their goodbyes as they looked backwards and scurried down the remaining portion of the Hardwood Floor to catch the trolley. Just like the Old Wise Lady of the Forest had advised, when they reached the end of the apple tree grove, the trolley came chugging in right on schedule.

The boys anxiously hopped on, squeezing through a sea of humanity and tightly clutching the nearest pole they could find. With the trolley more than at capacity, the doors smashed shut forcing a massive cramping of nervous bodies twitching for space and air. The dark shadows around the city of Eastern Paranoia could be seen on the outlying hillside.

Albert had an inquisitive smile molded firmly in position as usual, in anticipation of yet another exciting journey. Wilber, on the other hand, had his neck slightly dislocated as he strained to look behind him where the loudest voice on the trolley was stationed. Often a little more than fidgety, Wilber preferred to focus his mind on searching for the truth and sorting out the facts in order to stay one step ahead.

Nobody on the trolley seemed too interested in settling down and all the nervous energy was increasingly overwhelming, to say the least. Through the exchanging of oncoming and outgoing passengers, there was a constant shifting of eyeballs that seemed to only intensify as the trolley neared the outskirts of Eastern Paranoia.

Passing half lit buildings barred up for the night, Albert surveyed that there were no trees, no billboards, no fire hydrants, no light poles, nor any telephone booths. All the necessary accessories of society were gone for the night, as if they had literally rolled the city up for the evening.

The trolley halted to make another pickup. This time it was an obnoxious loud mouth who staggered down the aisle with his face slightly out of proportion and eyes keenly fixated on Wilber. The man laughed vulgarly, looking around to get the approval of his fellow Paranoians.

Albert ignored him and continued looking wide eyed out the window, noticing that even the telephone poles were taken out of inventory for the night. "Hey

Wilber, sorry to report that I think we are out of luck for finding any telephones, at least for tonight."

The conductor then announced loudly over the intercom, "First courtesy stop in two minutes. Now entering Eastern Paranoia."

The Paranoians on board slouched deeply into their seats, trying to remain inconspicuous. Many of the outsiders blinked timidly as the trolley penetrated the gloominess on the edge of the city.

Albert and Wilber tightly gripped the pole, trying to desperately hang on and keep their balance as the trolley jostled them back and forth. Suddenly they were knocked off kilter by a man from behind who wedged his way between them. He was dressed in a long black overcoat and detective hat and rudely shoved a crossword puzzle in Albert's face.

The Puzzler sputtered, "Let's see if you can help me out with this puzzle. How much do you really know about Eastern Paranoia, gentlemen? 16 Across: What makes your heart tick?"

Wilber eagerly leaned in and surveyed the puzzle. "Time!" he blurted out as if he were on some kind of game show.

"Right you are, young man," complimented The Puzzler. "Very impressive. Ok now, 5 Down and starts with the letter P: Facial lines of protruding attitudes and a very common theme around these parts."

"Paranoia, no doubt," Albert delivered.

"That's correct, sir and don't ever forget it. Ok, 22 Across ending with the letter C: Various disorders of the nervous system often accompanied by severe irrationality."

"Neurotic!" Wilber snapped, looking over his shoulder at some moving shadows.

"Very good, pencil neck!" The Puzzler teased. "And remember this, 41 Across starting with the letter I: To mentally attack with an offensive measure of forceful logic."

The Puzzler leaned way in on Wilber and bore down hard, "Come on, son. Hurry up!"

Wilber wilted away and shrugged his shoulders.

"Intimidate!!" The Puzzler shouted, stretching out the veins in his long neck.

Albert and Wilber backed off a couple feet as it was now getting very uncomfortable.

The Puzzler dialed up another one as he poked the crossword puzzle hard with his pencil. "36 Down, 5 letters and starts with S: It's against the law to do this in Eastern Paranoia—a slight hint of happiness accompanied by a furling of the lips in a very offensive manner."

"Smile?" Wilber guessed while trying his best not to smirk.

"Right you are, genius boy." Now here's one for you mister, as he turned and faced Albert abruptly.

As the trolley came to a halt and the doors slid open, Albert jerked away from The Puzzler and joked,

"Now, here's one for you, buddy: What has 2 letters and means exit?"

"GO, that's what!" Albert yelled back sarcastically as he grabbed Wilber by his arm, pulling him through a crack in the closing doors, quickly leaping off the trolley to safety.

They landed on the sidewalk and walked briskly in the opposite direction of the trolley, finding cover under a cafe awning to gather their thoughts. The streets seemed to be blanketed in a quiet and spooky aftermath where the only sound heard was that of chattering teeth. Dodging carefully down the sidewalk, looking carefully up each alley they crossed, everything seemed to be darkened by the tall buildings which shaded the face of the moon.

Albert broke the silence, "Hate to say this but if we're still here at daybreak, we may never have a chance to leave."

Wilber looked up for the first time in many sidewalk lines and agreed, "Yeah, these folks are really super desperate."

Albert traded glances with a character that wormed his way down a crooked alley. "Let's just follow this main arterial a piece until we get back into the moonlight and we'll be in better shape, I think."

The two of them beat it down the gloomy sidewalk with strides covering more than the recommended minimum. Any Paranoians they encountered were trying madly to just blend into the blemishes of the litter filled doorways of abandoned buildings. Out of sight, out of mind, so they say.

Up ahead in the town square, a preacher scurried across the street ringing a bell loudly to summon his pig who had barged wildly into a funeral procession of frightened marchers. The grievers, still in a constant hum, turned in the direction of the undertaker and followed him up the nearby alley to the graveyard.

As Albert and Wilber sauntered up to an intersection, Wilber was overtaken by a premonition. "Albert, I have a strong feeling we should go right here, up Vexation Drive."

"Are you positive, Wilber?" Albert stressed, trying in vain to make out the distorted figures peering back at him through the drug store windows.

As they turned the corner, they stopped in their tracks for a second. Up ahead, a Messenger Boy was exchanging conversation with a standard looking middle-aged Paranoian, holding on tightly to his sales briefcase. His face was extra shiny and his eyes alarmingly simple, void of any character and soul. A stiffly starched white shirt and tie gave him that certain safe and conservative factory appearance so apparent in this city.

Albert and Wilber made their way toward them, hopeful of getting information but being careful not to scare them off. The salesman and Messenger Boy were so engrossed in their transaction, they scarcely noticed as Albert and Wilber slowly approached from the darkness.

The salesman turned and greeted them, extending a pamphlet to Albert about purchasing a cemetery plot in the eternally beautiful Sunny Side Estates.

"Ah, no thank you sir," Albert shrugged, handing it quickly back. "No plans for that anytime soon. We just want to get home, that's all."

Wilber had already started interrogating the Messenger Boy. "What kind of material do you read here anyway and why isn't anybody normal?"

"Of course you must first understand that I cannot answer either of those questions," the Messenger Boy relayed, resting his head on the side of an old brick building. "But I can tell you that Eastern Paranoia is the only life we know, unfortunately."

"That's exactly right," butted in the salesman. "We'd love to have change but Voltage Control has taken over our fair city."

"Who?" Albert inquired, leaning in more closely.

The Messenger Boy looked around in all directions and whispered, "Voltage Control, the mad scientist of society, Professor Clodhopper and his magnificent crew, true masterminds."

"Where at?" Wilber wanted to know.

"Out on the eastern hillside of the city," the Messenger Boy replied back softly. "We can't get close enough though."

He then chalked out some details on the sidewalk. "Listen closely. I know of a small band of those who are seeking out Voltage Control—the Reminiscence Expedition. Look here. Just follow this road until you hit Focal Street. Turn right and you will be entering Melancholy Square. There will be benches there. Sit across from the lady in the black veiled face. She'll lead you to the meeting if you tap both feet, off beat. Remember, both feet, off beat."

"And another thing," reminded the cemetery peddler, "forget you ever saw me or I'll have to sell one of these plots to myself." He then doffed his checkered hat and was back out on the job.

The Messenger Boy stretched out his hand and received his customary tip. "Thank you and good luck. Now, if they doubt you, tell them I sent you." He then flipped his tip happily in the air and took off on his scooter.

Albert and Wilber filed on, determined to figure out this strange place. "Do you suppose we should dare check it out, Wilber?" asked Albert.

"It's all beyond me," Wilber reflected. "Everything here is so distant. How do you know who wears a mask and who doesn't?"

They continued on as instructed, not really being able to answer their own questions. When Focal Street had been reached, they hung a right. Down the street, the village clock sounded abruptly across Melancholy Square. Sure enough, seated at the end of the last bench in the square was the veiled woman the Messenger Boy had indicated. Perhaps the Old Wise Lady's sister she had referred to.

"Let's wait a bit to give her the secret signal," Albert recommended as they sauntered nonchalantly over to their assigned bench. They sat across from the woman for a few minutes taking in the air of Paranoia that drifted and hung so heavily and motionless.

Albert began tapping both feet in an off beat rhythm in an anxious effort to signal the black-veiled woman. After looking the terrace surroundings over, she gave a slight nod, got up and moved slowly across the green to an old factory. She vanished down a long assortment of stairs as Albert and Wilber trailed behind.

At the bottom, she cracked open a door under a factory and motioned the boys in. The room was cloudy with dust and steam and the lighting was very dim and hazy. The veiled woman then slid back out into the cold, nervous air without speaking to anyone or anyone speaking out at all. Aisles of folding, aluminum chairs lined the room where downtrodden and motionless figures anxiously awaited the meeting to start.

Albert planted himself next to a weary-eyed wanderer dressed in nightshade colors that would lose him to the night. His generic, familiar face seemed so obedient and alert that it hardly seemed Paranoian.

Just then, a bright light hit the wall outside. Everyone suddenly ducked down momentarily until the searchlight passed. Shrilling sighs could be heard from the women and children as they rose again when they felt it was safe.

The black-veiled woman slipped back in the door, barring it behind her and took position at a chalkboard in the front of the room. She then lifted her veil and pulled off a mask, revealing none other than Mr. Pattison, Commander of the Reminiscence Expedition, smiling sternly behind his toothpick.

He belted out, "That was the Urgent Agents of the Paranoian Forces from Voltage Control. Now, everybody as a whole, I want you to know, we shall find eternity, win back our dignity and rebuild a new society. The Reminiscence Expedition will seek and overtake Voltage Control before it's too late!"

The commander then chalked out the plan for the night on the blackboard.

Number 1: Forget your name.

Number 2: Always turn right when a patrolman looks left.

Number 3: Never have more than 3 people from the expedition together at once. Looks too suspicious and organized.

Number 4: If any of you do spot Voltage Control, don't try anything alone. Alert me immediately before taking any action.

Number 5: Stay alert at all times and use your walkie-talkies efficiently and quietly.

"Ok," concluded the commander, "Now that we've covered the basics, remember to pretend that you are only aimless Paranoians, correct?"

"Wrong!" spurted a distorted face prevailing from the back of the room behind Albert and Wilber.

The commander abruptly shined his flashlight on the face. "What is your name and where are you from, son?"

"Edgar! And I'm not from anywhere anymore," Edgar droned dully, straining through the smoke to see.

Wilber elbowed Albert softly in the ribs. They tried to remain at ease, even though most of the room was engaged in hushed snickering at the sight of this strange and distorted boy.

The commander sharply reprimanded the room. "Don't ever laugh! You'll give yourselves away and find yourself in jail." The momentary conglomeration of silliness had died down and the commander peered into the back bodies of the room. "Anyone else from some other place?"

At first, it seemed best to remain silent and hope that their distinctive facial features wouldn't be noticed. But it seemed like a great sum of piercing eyeballs were beaming in their direct vicinity so Wilber first raised his hand and then Albert followed.

"Oh them," Edgar blurted. "They're from another planet!"

Chairs rattled in nervousness until Wilber stood up and retracted the statement. "I'm afraid Edgar is mistaken. We're both in actuality from Centrifugal Drive in Suburbia Heights in a parallel universe, we've been told."

The commander held his hands up in the air, motioning the crowd to simmer down. "That's alright, they're with me, folks. I've checked them out and they are very smart explorers, indeed. I feel they can be very helpful to us and may in fact be way more open minded than any of you in this room. They just might bring some new ideas to the table so listen up to what they have to say out there tonight. It might do us all a little good."

"Now, let's please welcome Albert and Wilber to our team tonight," continued the commander, chomping down on his toothpick. The room offered up an obligatory, light applause and then Commander Pattison outlined, "As you might not be aware of, at Voltage Control they are devising improved techniques to completely control us through very specifically pointed subliminal telecommunication." He paused for a moment while he scanned the crowd to make sure everyone was dialed in.

"You see, by transmitting subliminal waves to us, they can constantly massage us with their orders and evil desires. We cannot really detect how, why or when we are summoned. But nevertheless, we do somehow hear them and therefore involuntarily do whatever we are told whenever they want."

"Sometimes, we might all receive the same signals simultaneously and yet at other times they definitely can control us individually. I need not emphasize enough that we are in extreme danger of being completely manipulated by these mad scientists of society." He stood looking back and forth at the forlorn frowns on everyone's face. "Now, you can obviously see the partial damage done to the city already — people commonly acting out in the same predictable patterns. This is why we must resist. With you, the Reminiscence Expedition, we can recapture our human dignity."

Commander Pattison held up his hand, pointing a big sausage sized finger out to the troops, "And remember," he pronounced, "be extremely careful out there."

Every person in that room absolutely trusted the commander, the mayor's right hand man and left handed son who happened to have an extremely oversized nose, excellent for finding out what one needs to know. He also had beady eyes tattooed on his eyelids so no one could take advantage of him when he had his eyes closed.

The commander bent over and pulled out packets of seeds from a burlap bag and passed them around. "One final message, eat these sanity seeds immediately upon spotting Voltage Control to fight off their power surges. Anyone who doesn't care to or need to participate in tonight's expedition may find the door at this time."

Amid shuffling of chairs and whispers, Albert and Wilber decided to strike out on their own and filed out into the Paranoian night with Edgar trailing behind.

"We just couldn't stay, Edgar," pointed out Wilber. "This Eastern Paranoia is nowhere."

"No kidding, huh?" grimaced Edgar. "Let's get out of here. Quick, follow me." Edgar led the way into the cold drift of the night as if by instinct. For several minutes, Albert and Wilber struggled to keep up with Edgar as he made his way through the rugged terrain for at least a good half mile out of town, finally halting at the edge of a river.

"I remember!" Edgar called out excitedly.

"Remember what, Edgar?" Albert pried.

Edgar explained, "I used to come here and watch Clown Benny play with his otter."

"You mean you know Clown Benny?" inquired Wilber. "We do too."

"Yeah," Edgar spouted. "He's one of the clown children that broke away from the Clown Army in the Hardwood Forest."

"You seem to know quite a lot about the Clown Army," Wilber cross examined. "What is their affiliation anyway?"

"I just can't make the connection," fizzed Edgar as he dashed off and trampled through the bushes. "Voltage Control! Voltage Control!"

Albert alerted Wilber, "Looks like Edgar might be onto something. We better follow him and fast."

Edgar was sliding uncontrollably down a steep bank with Albert and Wilber doing their best to maneuver behind him. At the bottom they hopped and stumbled sideways toward the dim image of Edgar who had taken a position behind a boulder. As Albert and Wilber crawled under cover toward Edgar they could now see that he was underneath a footbridge with high, shiny handrails and cyclone fencing.

Albert puffed heavily, "You knew this was here all along, Edgar? Why did you take off so fast?"

Edgar panted, "Didn't want to forget. Used to sit here and watch the Clown Army visit Voltage Control." Edgar pointed out beyond the end of the bridge and up a cliff, "Up there!"

"Ok then. We'll follow you," gestured Wilber as the search now took on a new force. They made their way up to the footbridge and scurried single file across the length of the bridge over the rapids of the river, being very careful to hug the edges of the cyclone fence and to stay low.

They had just finished crossing the footbridge when their ears fuzzed in tones of high, electrical power buzzes. Searchlights combed down from the cliff above them. The three quickly vanished down a bank under the bridge and into a thicket of bushes.

"I can feel the power surge from here," Wilber grimaced as he held his head, crawling on his stomach a little closer to peek through the bushes up at Voltage Control.

"If we could just get in there, we'd be heroes," Wilber motioned as he and the rest lay there trembling. The pressure had become so intense that the three of them had nearly driven themselves into a frenzy.

"Hold on, hold on," Albert briefed with caution. "We haven't actually even seen anything just yet. Let's at least calm down a little until then, ok boys?"

"Right you are, Albert," reasoned Wilber. "Hey, we've got to take our sanity seeds now to endure the power of Voltage Control. Who's got them anyway?"

"In sack, blowing away," Edgar pointed out. "I'll get them!"

"Wait!" snapped Albert, pulling Edgar back into the bushes. "Only one of us should go and I think it should be Wilber. He's much smaller than any of us and therefore has far less matter that can be detected by their radar."

By this time, the wind had picked up dramatically, blowing the packet of seeds even closer to the base of Voltage Control. So off was Wilber into the night, on the trail of the blowing sack of sanity seeds, so desperately needed. It was all Wilber could do to keep from screaming as the mounting pressures became quite real. Wilber made the brave decision to break from a crawl to a sprint and ran as quickly as he could ahead, diving for the sack and smothering it as he lay in exhaustion.

He grabbed a handful of sanity seeds and gobbled them down to contain the pressure and extremity of insanity. He then executed a barrel roll into some tall grass and weeds and rested for a couple minutes to catch his breath and regain his composure. After a couple minutes, Wilber's head seemed to be maintaining at a satisfactory level as he tried hard to make out the figures in the shadows of the basement window at Voltage Control. A couple more seeds down the hatch and Wilber couldn't help but move in a little more.

He crawled even closer to the window and was able to make out a silhouette of a figure in a lab coat who surely had to be Professor Clodhopper. He was laughing wildly with horse like jaws as he experimented in his lab.

During this time span, Albert and Edgar had grown restless, very concerned for Wilber's safety and down right delirious. Darting toward Wilber and the seeds of sanity, they reached Wilber and extracted a double dose of seeds. Laying in the grass, they did their best to remain perfectly still for a couple minutes until the seeds started to calm them all down.

Wilber wheeled around in the grass, tugging the others by their shirts. "We need to leave now. This is insanely dangerous," he whispered emphatically.

He led the way back through a set of trees as the radar from Voltage Control rotated high overhead with a pitch that was nearly unbearable. It had become apparent to Wilber that if he and the others didn't get off the grounds immediately, they would surely be detected. They high-tailed it out of there and darted back in the direction of the bridge, sliding down an embankment to a heart thumping rest, straining their necks up to see if they had been spotted.

The radar scanner was now in full rotation as it cast a siren over the controlled area. Suddenly a bigger than life sized monitor lit up on the side of the building, flashing a picture of Albert, Wilber and Edgar. They eyeballed themselves up on the screen in shock and listened to their hearts throbbing out of control over the p.a. system.

It had become more than obvious that they needed to pick up their frozen bodies and make a move for it. Albert felt a sudden surge of adrenaline and pulled the other two to their feet. They all knew what had to be done and with Albert leading the way, they slipped from view of the camera into the blackness again and down the long stairwell leading from Voltage Control.

Gaining momentum, they increased their strides through the bushes and out of sight, making their way down to the foot of the icy, metal bridge where they had so foolishly crossed earlier. Like the pulsating drums of the Paranoian soldiers and their hound dogs now on the march, the three boys briskly hustled to safety across the bridge and scaled the foggy hillside down into the outskirts of Eastern Paranoia.

The next half mile went so fast and in such a haze, they could scarcely even remember their daring escape. It's as if they were on auto-pilot or something, as if they had been lifted by a magic force of some kind who was watching over them. The combination of pure adrenaline and sanity seeds got them back into the outskirts of town before they knew it. Whoever would guess that the town of Eastern Paranoia would be such a welcome sight?

Leaning up against the side of an abandoned warehouse, they caught their breath as they contemplated their next maneuver. They all tried their best not to make eye contact with anyone who passed and slipped around the corner into a dark alley where they felt less vulnerable.

They were waiting impatiently for the crowds to pass when they were jolted by a sudden bicycle skid behind them. Whipping around, they were greeted by the Messenger Boy.

"Hello again," he delivered. "Didn't mean to scare you but I heard you guys have been spotted and will soon be exiled. I presume you would like to leave Eastern Paranoia?"

"Believe me," Albert obliged, looking back and forth at Wilber and Edgar, "we've wanted to since the very moment we got here. But how?"

"Right now," the Messenger Boy shot back, "by subway."

Albert and Wilber traded questions simultaneously, "The Subway To The Inner Fields of Self Identity?!"

"Precisely. That would be the one," assured the Messenger Boy as he moved aside a huge garbage container and squatted down in the alley, pulling off a manhole cover. "Hurry up and follow me down, gentlemen," he directed as he led the way down the spiraling ladder. After several rungs in the darkness, they touched down into a marble lined hallway.

When their eyesight adjusted to the darkness, they could see that Edgar was not present. They peered up into the hole of dim light where Edgar spoke to them tearfully, "I must go back now to the Old Wise Lady Of The Forest. Write me, ok?"

The sentiments were returned and now their attention was quickly directed through the marble corridor leading up to a ticket window.

"This is it, Wilber! This is it. We're going home now, just like Grandfather Genius had promised." He squinted as they drew closer and read the sign.

Entrance

Subway To The Inner Fields of Self Identity

Albert and Wilber turned to the Messenger Boy with deep gratitude, feeling chilled with inspiration as they bellied up to the ticket window and took a deep breath.

CHAPTER SEVEN

SUBWAY TO THE INNER
FIELDS OF SELF IDENTITY

The ticket window was unmanned this late at night, Wilber surmised, as it was now getting close to midnight. He studied the regulations and schedule for the subway and how to select your destination. Evidently, it was computerized once you boarded. Wilber punched one button for Children and another for Senior Citizens and snagged the tickets as they were dispensed from the contraption.

After exposing a pair of necessary smiles into the monitor, Wilber led the way through the turnstiles and they filed into a sound proofed waiting room which was lined in deep, white velvet and fun mirrors, including one that would show only your skeleton. Maybe this was not just for entertainment but maybe a security system?

"You sure this subway goes to our vicinity, Albert?"

"Positive, more than positive."

"Wonder where it stops? And why don't we know about it?"

"Well Wilber, that remains to be seen. But I tell you, it's almost like I know. I can't quite pinpoint it but I've got that notion, got that crazy notion, like I've been here before."

Boarding lights started throbbing and a partition whined as it opened into conjunction with the subway doors. A supervisor who had been standing by a computer near the subway controls, ushered them in. He led them down a long tubular aisle where capsules lined either side. "Two-man, four-man or a six-man enclosure, gentlemen? How's this one for just the two of you?" He handed them a pamphlet and advised, "Read this very carefully, fasten yourselves in securely and have fun!"

Albert slid himself into the capsule booth closest to the wall. The overhead was clear glass and you could vividly see the Eyeglass Tunnel above. The supervisor winked safely, inflating the pressurized door and then retreated to the controls where he eyed the departure time.

Wilber studied the pamphlet directions intensely for selecting their destination on the computer attached to the arm rest. S-U-B-U-R-B-I-A H-E-I-G-H-T-S was dialed in for the city and C-E-N-T-R-I-F-U-G-A-L D-R-I-V-E for the station stop. "There," Wilber stated proudly, "That should do it."

"Nicely done, Wilber. Hey, it says here that this subway runs at a superlative speed that is faster than the speed of thought. Let's figure this thing out."

The two leafed through the pamphlet, feeding various combinations and factors into the computer on the arm rest.

"Albert, according to my calculations, we will get home around 1:00 on Sunday afternoon! How is that even possible? Faster than the speed of thought is for real, I guess. Hold on to your hat."

A surging sensation of solar sunbeams filled the Eyeglass Tunnel overhead, sending extremely stimulating shocks and spirits of vibrations throughout the interior of the subway as they were now only moments from takeoff.

A man seated across the aisle from Wilber in a low-brimmed hat drooped his face and let out a foot long snore, dropping his newspaper to the floor. The wavy face of the Subway Captain flashed over the closed circuit screen. "Please stand by for departure and prepare yourself for an impactful force."

Everyone tightened up and braced their feet and then with a rearing thrust, the subway shot off, leaving Albert isolated in some strange kind of suspended state, withstanding a tremendous G-force.

The active rays of the EyeGlass Tunnel penetrated fully into the passenger enclosure, sharpening his mental awareness as the subway soared through the Inner Fields Of Self Identity at intensities previously unknown.

Albert had seemingly left the vicinity, chatting within himself. There was an echoing over and over in his head abut this mysterious familiarity. Only questions though, no answers and certainly no sense of his body as he slipped further and further away into peaceful oblivion.

Wilber could scarcely even glance over at Albert as he was so personally overtaken by the powerful force of the subway. It seemed easier to just let go and as he did, an overwhelming sense of the deepest love ever imaginable filled his little soul as he floated effortlessly. He was now completely void of all earthly things as he enjoyed this blissful state and became as one with the sunbeams of the subway, so easily going with the flow and losing all sense of time and space.

They both hung in this suspended state of transition seemingly for infinity.

Suddenly, the supervisor's voice blurted out on the intercom over the silent screams of the passengers, "Attention! Attention please. We are now approaching the Suburbia Heights station at a depth of minus 3 degrees to compensate for the curvature of the earth. We ask you please to now brace yourselves for arrival and decompression. Thank you."

As the subway whirred loudly and decelerated, Wilber gently re-entered into his body and pondered, "How could we be here already?" He did a double take as he checked and re-checked his watch, extremely alarmed to discover it was 1:00 Sunday afternoon.

Albert sat perplexed as he came to, being temporarily neutralized inside the pressurized capsule for a minute before finally maintaining a sense of proper stability.

The door to their capsule was deflated by the supervisor who waited by patiently and professionally for the two to gain their senses. Albert and Wilber struggled to their feet and fought to gain their balance and then stepped out slowly, following the supervisor down the aisle to the subway exit.

The supervisor then led them down the end of the corridor of the station and paused for a moment. "This is your exit to Suburbia Heights, gentlemen. Follow me if you will."

The boys trailed behind him closely and were led up a long flight of darkened stairs, listening to the supervisor's voice carefully. "I can actually still remember the first, last and only time we've ever made a stop here, many decades ago. It seems like some young boy stumbled upon us while eating a muffin or something." He then doffed his cap and stroked back his gelled hair before trying to budge open the cobweb laced door to the outside.

He struggled mightily, huffing away with all his force but could not get the door to budge a bit. He tried again to no avail and was quickly losing strength. "I'm afraid she's stuck, boys. Mind if you give me a hand?"

Albert snapped out of his trance. "Here, excuse me for a second, sir." He stepped back and ran full force into the door, throwing a cross body block, crashing into the daylight.

The supervisor clapped heartily. "Good piece of work, Albert! Just like in your old high school glory days as a linebacker, huh?" He chuckled as he was closing the door. "Well, good luck getting home safely, gentlemen and good day."

Albert looked up from the ground, scanning the surroundings underneath an abandoned railroad bridge. They were surrounded by an overgrown grassy field enclosed by a high, barbed-wire fence. NO TRESPASSING signs were posted everywhere around the perimeter.

"Albert, look over there!" Wilber pointed at a receptionist sitting attentively at her desk in the middle of the field. "I'll be right back. Better ask her where the heck we are."

"You do that," Albert strained from his inner voice, trying desperately to regain his backsliding senses and why he had nearly fallen asleep on the subway. What was that? He knew that his senses were not just tricking him anymore. He whispered, "Is this the place I played on that November afternoon when I was only seven? By The Subway To The Inner Fields of Self Identity?"

He was trying to relive this déjà vu fragment and sat down by a nearby stream, thinking back and plopping rocks into the stream to relax. Was it here? He viewed his reflection in the water, staring back at himself again and again until the reflection soon molded into that of a small child's face. He sat up and took one last look, reassuring himself that he was really ok and went over to meet Wilber who was jogging his way with directions.

Albert had an epiphany. "Wilber! Wilber," Albert barely croaked out, not yet knowing what to say as he vividly felt as though he had something important to explain. "Come on, Wilber. Follow me," Albert insisted, leading the way along the stream to where he spotted something under some bushes.

It was an old stick horse. "Wow," trembled Albert, now realizing so clearly just what the significance was. "Do you know what this is, Wilber?"

"Wow, what? It's just an old stick horse, that's all," shrugged Wilber.

"Yeah, my old horse," Albert winked as he dropped it down to the ground and rode it along the fence line for a few feet.

Wilber laughed and followed Albert. "That's pretty cool, Albert. Pretty cool."

"Hey Wilber, I bet you there's a hole under the fence somewhere up here just a bit, as I recall. Come on."

"What makes you think that anyway?"

"Don't know," Albert yelled back, feeling that lively presence again that he had been here before and this was familiar territory.

"There it is!" flashed Wilber, scampering ahead. "Over here!" He squeezed under to the other side and lifted the bottom of the fence up higher for Albert to get through. Albert crawled underneath to the other side and slowly stood up a little unsteadily, dusting himself off.

"You sure look pale, Albert," observed Wilber. "What's happening to you, anyway?"

"Wilber, I do agree something strange is happening to me."

"What is it? What do you mean?"

"Not sure yet. I'll try to explain it in a little while. Let's just get home for now, ok?"

"Oh, come on Albert," Wilber pleaded. "You can tell your best friend. Is this some kind of déjà vu or something?" Wilber tried his best to find the answer in Albert's eyes.

Albert gulped and took a deep breath, trying to muster a more stable facial expression that wouldn't worry his little buddy. "Ok Wilber," Albert confessed. "I almost fell asleep on the subway, didn't I? And the other day too, I think."

Wilber stared blankly trying to absorb the information and offer some comfort. "Albert, don't beat yourself up. That subway was something altogether different. I went into some kind of weird state myself. I wouldn't worry about it."

"You're probably right, Wilber. We can talk about it later."

"Hey wait a minute," spouted Wilber, stopping in his tracks. "What are we going to tell everyone about where we've been since we went to the circus Saturday morning?"

Albert pondered for a moment. "You're right. According to the Star Zip Trip rules, we were supposed to come back the day before we left. Maybe Newton did but I think that we came back and lived Saturday all over again, not Friday. So, here we are the next day and it's now Sunday. Let's just be vague and say the experiment for the Star Zip Trip went slightly awry."

"Right," Wilber nodded in agreement. "Just be rather vague until they get bored and laugh and start talking about their golf game or favorite recipes or something."

Albert chuckled into his knuckles. "Sounds simple enough. I'd kind of like to keep this whole thing a secret anyway. Nobody would ever believe us anyhow. You think we'll ever get back there again, Wilber?"

But Wilber didn't really hear Albert. He was only partially able to surface from his thoughts, weighing questions heavily about the reruns of the day, featuring The Subway To The Inner Fields of Self Identity.

They turned and clawed their way up the hillside of Suburbia Heights toward Centrifugal Drive. As they grew more and more excited about getting home, they gained speed and endurance, finally reaching the summit at the dead end of their street. Funny, all those years, they never would have dared disobey the No Trespassing signs and dangerous descent to this forbidden area that was fenced in. Right now, all they could focus on was getting back to reality, into a warm house, loved ones they knew, fresh clothes, a relaxing bath and a nice hot meal. Just the basics that everyone seems to take for granted, seemed so welcoming after this surreal sojourn of a weekend. It had been a doozy. A real doozy.

"Wilber, you know this has all been pretty heavy, yes? I mean, I kind of hate to see it all end so suddenly," stuttered Albert. "This was the journey of all journeys, for sure."

"Know what you mean." Wilber whole heartedly agreed. "The subway sure got us here in a hurry, before I was quite ready. It seems like only a few minutes ago, we were trapped in Eastern Paranoia. I'll have to do some ultra serious research on the theory of quantum time and space for my science thesis. This could be just the ticket I need to get into that university program next summer."

As they climbed over the wooden traffic barrier at the end of Centrifugal Drive, Wilber spotted Newton down the street a few houses. "Hey Newton, over here!" Wilber waved his hands back and forth over his head.

Newton N. Newton the 3rd was trying out his newest invention of a Quadricycle, which he had customized specifically for Albert. He quickly hummed up the street to meet up with them.

"When did you get it running?" grinned Wilber.

"Just 11:00 this morning," answered Newton as he opened the passenger doors.

"11:00 this morning!" Albert gasped. "What time is it anyway?"

"Almost 1:30. I was just testing out this new vacuum whistle I came up with. It operates on a range of silent vapors that transform into combustible frequencies of motion." He beamed proudly behind the computerized dashboard. "Hop in, hop in!"

Albert and Wilber slid in as Newton looked them over head to toe. "What in the neighborhood of misfortune happened to you guys after you launched off the Star Zip Trip? An awful lot of people began to have their doubts about your safety. That is until about an hour ago when some full-blooded clown kid wrote Maid Martha and Wilber's parents a note saying you were safe and on your return home. It was signed

Clown Benny. He must have been a real, authentic clown because he didn't have a tongue."

Newton engineered the Quadricycle down Centrifugal Drive beyond Wilber's house. Wilber panicked slightly. "Newton, you just went past my house!"

"So?" Newton winked teasingly. "Guess what? We're all going over to Mr. Silverton's house for a welcome home party. The whole town is very anxious for your arrival."

As they reached Mr. Silverton's, Albert and Wilber exchanged a pair of nervous glances as the Quadricycle turned up the long estate driveway. Mr. Silverton waddled hastily down the driveway, leading the pack of neighbors, the press and special town dignitaries who all quickly closed in on the boys.

Mr. Silverton was first to welcome home the boys. "Albert! Wilber! So good to see you boys are safely home. The elves have been tireless in eating my prize roses in your absence," he joked. Mr. Silverton swiftly began to talk more business as lightbulbs flashed from the cameramen and reporters leaned in for more information, seeing who could be first to break the story in tonight's news and tomorrow morning's newspaper in the Post-Intelligencer.

"Albert! You're seven minutes late for lunch," complained Martha the Maid from under her new hat, tugging at him and trying her best to pull him through the crowd.

"Martha, please!" Albert pleaded, trying to tolerate the clashes of reporters' determined glasses, questionable syllables and masses of camera flashes.

Wilber was unexpectedly smothered from behind by his father, dressed smartly in a fresh, new suit. He said in his usual professional, deep voice, "I must say, I am overwhelmingly pleased to have you back safely, out of harm's way, son."

"You bet, dad. It's nice to be back and I now have some very exciting new research to report on for my science thesis!"

Photographers dodged in and out of the scene. "A picture over here, you two. Now down here. Now look up. Look over here sideways, and give us your best smile. Once again please? Splendid. Thank you so much." They all jostled for prime position, hoping to get that prized, front page photo for tomorrow morning. Reporters rapidly scratched out facts on their notepads as they listened intently to Wilber's account, which by the way, was going perfectly as planned — very subdued, fast and foggy.

The sun was struggling to peek out behind some cracks in the clouds as the party had now reached the pillared steps near the back of the mansion. For the most part, the initial impact of re-acquaintances had simmered down except for a few sideline hand shakers. Mr. Silverton announced that drinks were now being served in the ballroom.

Inside, the party was particularly typical for Suburbia Heights, where nearly everyone was worth more than themselves. The mingling of characters began slipping from one clique to another, where hot discussions persisted on the serious threat to the acting field.

Albert had slipped away into the pantry by himself, happily leaving the hubbub of self absorption behind. There just didn't seem to be any way of waiting any longer for what he had to do — get back to the subway and solve this dilemma once and for all.

Meanwhile, the festivities had totally developed into full fledged social mania. As Albert slipped out the pantry door to the back porch, strains of slow laughter rose from the lawn chairs scattered around the pools.

Albert had departed the view of most after a quick and spontaneous newspaper interview on the back patio. He stealthily moved into the shadows and walked around the back of the house into the rose garden to get some quiet.

Wilber too had left the ballroom and despite his efforts to locate Albert, it was to no avail. Wilber singled out Newton in a sea of disinterested faces near the study. "Hey Newton, have you seen Albert?"

"Sorry Wilber," responded Newton, who was sitting by himself in a leather executive chair at Mr. Silverton's desk. "Haven't seen him in several minutes. Last time I saw Albert, he was exchanging two bit conversation with a reporter and heading out the pantry."

"I'll check it out, Newton. I have a feeling where he might be. Meet us out front, ok?" Wilber drew away from the friction of the party and headed out the back pantry door. He headed out behind the pool fencing and down a steep, rolling slope to the rose garden and sure enough, found Albert perched against a chestnut tree.

"Hi Wilber," droned Albert.

"Albert, is there something wrong?"

Albert popped a blade of grass into his mouth and confided, "It's about that place, Wilber. You know, the subway. I have to go back and get this thing figured out."

Wilber could feel the shakiness in Albert's voice and completely understood. "I think we'd better leave. Let's sneak out of the party."

So, in single file, they crept behind the tallest rose bushes and thickest tree trunks, along the iron fence and down the sidewalk to Albert's garage next door. Newton awaited in his Quadricycle.

Albert trembled a little bit as he was now realistically anticipating a return to the subway. This was about to get very real. With everyone now aboard, Newton N Newton guided the machine out into the late afternoon sun and headed down Centrifugal Drive toward the cliff at the dead end. Neither Wilber or Newton dared speak as Albert tried to explain over and over again that his conscience was fluttering with some profound, indelible memory of the past. His long, white hair whistled in the wind and it was all too soon when Newton slowed the Quadricycle down at the end of street by the traffic barrier.

"Good luck, Albert. Wilber, I hope at day's end, we may call a meeting," Newton suggested in his nasal tone as he extended the official Space Scout's salute. "To the future."

As soon as Newton hummed away, Albert and Wilber eagerly exchanged ideas for their plan, sliding uncontrollably down the steep hillside towards the abandoned subway station. And to think that Albert had lived here for the past seventy years and had no idea whatsoever that this subway lay at the bottom of the ravine, so close to his home, yet so far away. But now it was time.

Once they landed on their backsides at the bottom, they scrambled through the brush toward the meadow and ran alongside the high cyclone fence trying to remember where the hole was. They scooted under the fence that Albert had somehow remembered, disregarded all the No Trespassing signs, followed an old path downstream and broke into an open field.

Wilber got excited when he realized where they were and led the way as they headed towards the partly secluded and vine smothered door to the station. With one last scan of the world behind them, Albert stepped in front of Wilber and yanked open the old door and they entered with equal excitement and apprehension.

Filing down a long, dark staircase and through a spider infested hallway, they hustled their way toward the boarded up ticket booth and turnstiles.

Welcome

Subway To The Inner Fields

Of Self Identity

CHAPTER EIGHT

THE RETURN

This time, Albert and Wilber, being the experienced troopers they were, fully knew what to expect. They were led into a white velvet, soundproofed waiting room and requested to relax and ready themselves for departure. They bathed in the tranquil ambience and beautiful light, cleansing their minds of all baggage and focusing deeply on nothing but positive thoughts for the journey ahead.

Eventually, a pleasantly plump man in an official blue suit entered the waiting room and motioned for them to follow. He led them through the subway tube to a four-man capsule that would give them plenty of room to stretch out. He then handed the instruction pamphlet to Wilber, who snatched it up right away, and then sealed the door shut. He offered a goodbye salute and wink to the boys and then merrily waddled back to his station.

Just like the time before, Albert took the window seat and Wilber settled into the aisle seat. A small boy with his face buried in a newspaper sat across from them. Albert looked up and down the aisle of the subway and took note that it was empty except for just the three of them. That struck him as a little odd.

Wilber knew exactly what to do and eagerly prepared to dial in the destination on the computer embedded in the arm rest. "What's our destination this time, Albert?"

Albert glared alarmingly into Wilber's eyes with absolute determination. "What else? The Inner Fields of Self Identity!"

The Subway Captain, noticing this most unusual destination pop up on his screen, made his way down the aisle and peeked into the capsule with a puzzled look of concern. He cracked open the door, introduced himself and wished them a very safe journey before closing up and inflating the pressurized capsule.

The subway started to idle at a much higher pitch and now they knew takeoff would be only moments away. In an instant, within a blinking thrust, the subway shot off like a bullet, leaving the boys' tummies in their throats. A massive flood of solar powered sunbeams filled their capsule and this time, feeling more like wily old veterans, they completely let go and became suspended in the vibrations.

Wilber managed to squeeze out a few words as he desperately hung on. "This is all so unreal, Albert."

But Albert couldn't manage to answer as he shakily fingered the computer panel, not so sure if this was a good idea after all and wondering if they should rethink their decision. Whatever it was that was eating at his mind, would soon be answered. He whimpered excitedly as he sunk back, intaking the magnificent rays and forces that were transmitting from the EyeGlass Tunnel overhead.

Albert studied the capsule more closely to try and quiet his mind. The padding of the capsule surrounding him had the appearance of brain cells that were connected to a network of wires that looked like blood vessels.

Albert locked into the frequency forces running through him and continued to get even more and more energized over the next few minutes, transcending chronological planes. As the subway gained more and more speed, the colors and vibrations pulsated wildly out of control. Albert clutched on tightly to the side of his seat as he felt a stiff jolt of power surge through his inner soul and body.

His head snapped back as the subway suddenly launched into hyperdrive. Albert was overwhelmed with a sensation of imperial, spiritual warmth as a lifetime of vivid memories flashed before him.

"Hey! Hey, you!"

Albert was alarmed by Wilber who was trying to gain the attention of the young child across from them, still buried in his newspaper.

Wilber pleaded once more. "Hey kid, you got the time?"

And so stood the incident, as the youngster pulled down the paper, catching Albert within the impact of a glance. For this child was no other than Albert, still but seven years old!!

"What is it, Albert?!" blared Wilber. Albert had slumped over in his chair and dropped to the floor in shock. Wilber could not reach him through the thick mind fog and what seemed to be a really bad movie playing out in super slow motion. Albert could scarcely hear Wilber's voice penetrating through the sound curtain. It seemed to be coming from far, far away — almost out of body or from some other dimension, from the other side.

Wilber fumbled over the controls on the computer trying to find a way to get Albert quickly back home to safety. He managed to alter the destination and quickly registered for a round trip from the Inner Fields of Self Identity back to Suburbia Heights.

As the subway came to a sudden stop at the next depot, Wilber broke out of his deep concentration and glanced over to the other seat but the boy had vanished. Wilber snapped around to look back down the corridor where he spotted the boy scurrying up some steps to an exit. He couldn't really get a clear look at him as the boy had his back turned.

Wilber leaned down and helped Albert struggle back into his seat. Over the next few minutes, Albert's mind was ablaze with a whirling elixir of mumbling, chuckling, distorted faces, the school bus, the park, the circus, the Hardwood Floor, Eastern Paranoia, the subway and his seven year old clone all tumbling around and around in his brain like loose tumbleweed.

The journey back to Suburbia Heights was very dreamy, gentle and tranquil, feeling as though they were floating through the tunnel in some kind of reverse, slow motion. Time passed along effortlessly in the stillness, like a feather drifting softly from the sky. Both Albert and Wilber completely surrendered their thoughts and all sense of consciousness, that suspended state that we all experience from time to time, somewhere between being almost asleep and dreams. Time stood still as the miles unfurled.

A hand grasped tightly onto Albert's arm but he wasn't the least bit startled. It was Wilber. Or was it?

"Wilber, is that you?" Albert squinted to get a closer look as he rose out of his slumber.

"Yes, it's me, Albert," Wilber comforted. "I think we're home now. Let's get you home to bed."

The Subway Captain deflated the pressurized door to their capsule and held an eyeglass up to his very enlarged eyeball. He examined Albert for a few seconds and recommended that Wilber take good care of him as he ushered them out.

The next few minutes were very fuzzy as Albert dogged along behind Wilber who assisted him off the subway and led him up the hallway steps into daylight, which was now dwindling in the last traces of this late autumn afternoon. Once again, Wilber called out loudly for Albert's attention but not to much avail.

Somehow, they managed to get up the hill to Centrifugal Drive as Albert had miraculously summoned enough inner drive and determination to make it to the top. Fortunately, Albert was fit as a fiddle for his age. Let's remember that.

The twilight of evening was setting in by the time they reached Albert's driveway. Wilber asked Albert if he would like to chase some elves tonight over at Mr. Silverton's. It was his way of pretending not to notice Albert's level of incompetency. It was also his hope that he could get Albert to snap out of it.

"Yeah, I would kind of like to," Albert weakly contemplated, "but I suppose I better just be by myself tonight, at least for a while."

With that said, Wilber gave his very best Space Scout salute and turned toward home with his hands buried deep in his pockets, gravely concerned for Albert's well being.

Martha was sound asleep in her official chair by the door as Albert came in the house, quietly ripping off some obligatory "How are you doings, good to be homes, and I'll see you in my dreams." He avoided bursting out in laughter over the bizarre events of the day and quietly slinked up the stairway to his room. Martha kept on rocking and scarcely even noticed, which was just fine by Albert. He really wanted no part of trying to explain what he had just been through or why he left his own party. He really just wanted to be alone now and collect his thoughts. This had been a very trying day.

Albert's bedroom seemed oddly peculiar, like seeing something for the first time, with a new set of eyes. The walls seemed a little tighter and the old fella looking back in the mirror looked extremely ragged. Eyes were a little off center too, come to think about it.

Albert plopped down in front of his bedroom window in his rocking chair and rocked back and forth to the beat of his heart. Surely he would find comfort in that. The hours rotated onward into the black mask of the night, Albert lost in his thoughts, constantly rewinding the day. Rewinding his life. The elves, for some weird reason, were not chattering tonight, so it was just as well that he wasn't out there anyway, chasing them.

After a few hours, as the night continued to unwind and Albert was able to rest his head, he got up slowly and moved over to his desk. He stared out the window, getting lost in his reflection and picked up a pencil.

Albert wrote virtually the whole night away into the dawn, carefully drawing and designing pictures and occasionally stopping to have a good, long look in the mirror. The face was still his, that's for sure, although he definitely did not feel like himself.

> *Seemingly, the subway holds the key*
> *To all the mysteries inside of me*
> *Please unlock this misunderstanding*
> *Let the wisdom cry out*
> *Just beyond a shout*
> *Just outside my window*
> *My memories dripping out*
> *So I tried my best to climb out of it*
> *But my mind was too short*
> *And the truth just wouldn't fit*
>
> *I feel like a tired river*
> *Narrowing the distance to the waterfall*
> *Making no last resistance*
> *No desperation at all*
> *Flowing freely, into the deep infinity*
> *Goodbye, I wave*
> *Slipping gently away*
> *Into this sweet senility*

"Time to get up, Albert!" ignited Martha the maid as she flung some good 'ol Dr. Corncob's Grits into the skillet.

Albert slowly lifted himself out of his rocker and leaned over, flipping on the radio (like every morning) to hear the announcer's voice. "Now, here's the tune of a lifetime, an oldie but a goodie! This request is dedicated this morning from Wilber to Albert, who can't make it to school today, on this fine Monday."

Albert seated himself back in front of the window, letting that sweet music that had blistered his ears since his youth, fully sink in. He stared blankly out the window at Wilber who waved to him from the bus stop down below, and hummed along with moistened eyes, to those words he would never forget.

Blueberry muffins are up a buck a pair
Newspapers bloom in Time Square
Time, time, time
That's a laugh and a half
Time is a common point of view -
So, here's looking at you

ABOUT THE AUTHORS

Starmel Spring (aka Richard Hodgert) and Leroy Henry met in the magical summer of 1967 when Leroy was the Hodgert family's paperboy. They became fast friends and soon discovered they had an affinity for the same kind of music, literature and humor.

Richard was raised in the Shoreline suburb of Seattle, Washington where he spent his entire life. He was a voracious writer with no bounds, whether it be song lyrics, poetry, or stories. In all rooms of his house, one could find mounds and scraps of paper with his creative burst of thoughts and unique outlook on the world. And it never stopped until his passing in 2013.

Leroy, a songwriter and producer, attended the University of Washington and enjoyed a career as a disc jockey in the 70's and early 80's at rock stations in

Seattle including KCMU, KZOK and KZAM. He then transformed his love for entertainment into the retail world as a music supervisor, curating songs for brands worldwide. Leroy was the founder and vice president of the music department at PlayNetwork in Redmond, Washington and currently acts as the Executive Producer of Global Starbucks, helping to create the in-store experience. He currently resides in Edmonds, Washington.

(Image on preceding page: Richard on the left, Leroy on the right. Image above: Leroy today.)

Visit our website at www.blueberrymuffins.org!

Made in the USA
Charleston, SC
22 June 2016